SLAPPY IN DREAMLAND

GOOSEBUMPS®
HALL OF HORRORS

#1 CLAWS!
#2 NIGHT OF THE GIANT EVERYTHING
#3 SPECIAL EDITION: THE FIVE MASKS OF DR. SCREEM
#4 WHY I QUIT ZOMBIE SCHOOL
#5 DON'T SCREAM!
#6 THE BIRTHDAY PARTY OF NO RETURN

GOOSEBUMPS®
MOST WANTED

#1 PLANET OF THE LAWN GNOMES
#2 SON OF SLAPPY
#3 HOW I MET MY MONSTER
#4 FRANKENSTEIN'S DOG
#5 DR. MANIAC WILL SEE YOU NOW
#6 CREATURE TEACHER: FINAL EXAM
#7 A NIGHTMARE ON CLOWN STREET
#8 NIGHT OF THE PUPPET PEOPLE
#9 HERE COMES THE SHAGGEDY
#10 THE LIZARD OF OZ

SPECIAL EDITION #1 ZOMBIE HALLOWEEN
SPECIAL EDITION #2 THE 12 SCREAMS OF CHRISTMAS
SPECIAL EDITION #3 TRICK OR TRAP
SPECIAL EDITION #4 THE HAUNTER

GOOSEBUMPS®
SLAPPYWORLD

#1 SLAPPY BIRTHDAY TO YOU
#2 ATTACK OF THE JACK!
#3 I AM SLAPPY'S EVIL TWIN
#4 PLEASE DO NOT FEED THE WEIRDO
#5 ESCAPE FROM SHUDDER MANSION
#6 THE GHOST OF SLAPPY
#7 IT'S ALIVE! IT'S ALIVE!
#8 THE DUMMY MEETS THE MUMMY!
#9 REVENGE OF THE INVISIBLE BOY
#10 DIARY OF A DUMMY
#11 THEY CALL ME THE NIGHT HOWLER!
#12 MY FRIEND SLAPPY
#13 MONSTER BLOOD IS BACK
#14 FIFTH-GRADE ZOMBIES
#15 JUDY AND THE BEAST

GOOSEBUMPS®

Also available as ebooks

ALSO AVAILABLE:

SLAPPY IN DREAMLAND

R.L. STINE

SCHOLASTIC INC.

Goosebumps book series created by Parachute Press, Inc.
Copyright © 2022 by Scholastic Inc.

ISBN 978-1-338-75216-8

10 9 8 7 6 5 4 3 2 1   22 23 24 25 26

Printed in the U.S.A. 40
First printing 2022

SLAPPY HERE, EVERYONE.

Welcome to My World.

Yes, it's *SlappyWorld*—you're only *screaming* in it! Hahaha!

Warning: Just because I'm so good-looking doesn't mean I'm not smart!

I'm so smart, I can spell my name *in the dark*! Hahaha.

I'm so smart, I can spell my name forward, backward, and *inside out*!

I know you're jealous of my good looks. When I look in a mirror, the mirror says, "Thank you!" Hahaha.

I'm so handsome, every time I look in a mirror, it's love at first sight!

Do you know who my dream date would be? Me! Hahahaha.

And speaking of dreams, here's a story about a boy named Richard Hsieh. Richard has a problem with nightmares. The problem is, he's having them day and night!

I think you'll like Richard's story. Mainly because it also stars a fabulous character—ME! Hahaha.

I'll promise you one thing—the story won't put you to sleep!

It's another dreamy tale from *SlappyWorld*!

1

Slappy stared across the table at me. His eyes gleamed under the lamplight, and his red-lipped grin made him look like he was happy to be here.

Maybe you'll think I'm weird. But that ventriloquist dummy is my best friend. Ever since Dad gave him to me for my twelfth birthday, we've been pals.

I keep Slappy with me wherever I go. I even took him to school once. Mom warned me not to, and she was right. Some kids in my classes laughed at me and made jokes about how I must be a dummy, too.

Not funny.

My name is Richard Hsieh, and I'm really not a weird dude. The truth is, I've always wanted a pet, and I'm allergic to dogs and cats.

So I guess Slappy takes the place of a pet for me.

My family moved to Russet Village less than a year ago, and I started at Russet Middle School last September. So I haven't had time to make real friends.

And I have to admit something about me. I'm shy. When I started at the new school, I had to fill out a questionnaire. You know. A lot of questions about what I like to do and what I don't like.

At the bottom, it said: *Can you describe yourself in one word?*

And that's what I wrote—*shy*.

I was going to write *awesome*. Just as a joke. But I thought whoever read my answers might take it seriously and think I'm stuck-up.

I looked at Slappy. Then down at the table.

I was doing a thousand-piece jigsaw puzzle with black-and-white pandas on it—no color—so it was really hard. "It's almost done. Only twelve pieces to go," I said.

Slappy grinned back at me. I really wished he could talk.

Dad keeps telling me to stop talking to the dummy all the time. He thinks it's too weird.

But Mom is a doctor, and she doesn't see any problem with it. "Lots of kids have imaginary friends they talk to," she told Dad.

"Sure. When they are *three*," Dad shot back.

"He can talk to Slappy all he wants," Mom said. "It's not like Richard imagines that Slappy is alive."

Dad shrugged, blew out a long whoosh of air, and left the room.

Dad is manager of the hardware store in town. A few days before my birthday, he found a beat-up suitcase in the back room of the store. He opened the case and found Slappy folded up inside it.

The dummy's gray suit was wrinkled, and his wooden head had scratches on it and a tiny chip missing from his nose. Dad asked the other store workers if they knew who had left the dummy there. No one had a clue.

So that's how Slappy became my birthday gift.

Mom and Dad washed him up before they let me have him. "He probably has lice or something," Dad said.

"What an evil grin," Mom said.

"It is *not* an evil grin," I said. "He's just smiling."

"It looks like he's smiling about something evil," Mom said. "Maybe you can practice with him, Richard. Practice making him talk. Work up a comedy act. That might be fun."

"I . . . I'm not very good with jokes," I told her.

Mom frowned at me. "But it might help build up your confidence," she said.

I wasn't sure about that. But I did like having Slappy with me. And maybe I did talk to him too often. But so what?

I had been staring at the black-and-white jigsaw puzzle so long, my eyes were starting to go blurry. "Just a few more pieces," I told Slappy.

But I felt a hand on my shoulder. "Get your coat, Richard," Mom said. "Dinner ran so long, we're late."

I looked up from the pandas. "Late?"

"Did you forget? You're coming with me to my lab tonight. It's Bring-Your-Kid-to-Work Day."

I dropped the puzzle piece in my hand and jumped up from the table. "Sorry, Mom. I'll get my coat."

"And how about some shoes?" she said. "Shoes might be good."

I hurried to my room to get my sneakers.

4

Mom runs an overnight sleep lab at the hospital. I guess people who have trouble sleeping come to her lab. I've never been there before.

I tied my sneakers. Then I pulled my jacket out of the front closet. "Is it okay if I bring Slappy?" I asked.

Mom squinted at me. "Slappy?"

"Yes. Is it okay if I bring him?"

She thought about it for a moment. "Sure," she said. "Bring him along. The more the merrier."

And that's when all the trouble started.

Mom's sleep lab has its own entrance at the side of the hospital. We walked down a brightly lit hallway. Then Mom pushed open the doors to the lab.

I blinked as my eyes adjusted to the dim gray light. I saw dark curtains and narrow beds and lots of computer equipment. The curtains formed a row of bedrooms, with a bed and a computer in each room.

People were already here. Some sat on their beds. Three of them stood in a corner, talking. They were all dressed in pajamas and robes. They turned as Mom and I walked in.

"Sorry I'm late," Mom said. "This is my son, Richard. And that thing he has draped over his shoulder is his dummy friend, Slappy."

"Slappy might give me nightmares!" a man called from one of the beds.

A few people laughed. Most of them looked pretty old to me. But I saw a couple of younger people, too.

"Don't say that," Mom said. "This is a no-nightmare zone, remember?"

A young man in a white lab uniform appeared

from a back room. He was tall and thin and had dark eyes and straight black hair pulled behind his head in a short ponytail.

"Hello, Doctor," he said. "This must be your son."

Mom introduced me and Slappy. "Richard, this is Salazar, my assistant," she said. "Salazar does all the hard work here. I just watch everyone sleep."

He chuckled. "Your mom is being modest," he said. He turned to my mother. "Only six here tonight. Mrs. Baker couldn't come in. I was just about to hook everyone up."

"I'll put Slappy in my office," Mom said. She pointed to the back room. Through the big window, I could see rows of computer monitors. "Then you can watch Salazar hook up the patients. He can explain what we do here."

She lifted Slappy off my shoulder. "Wow. He's heavier than I thought."

The dummy's eyelids lowered. I laughed. "Slappy knows he's in a sleep lab!"

Shaking her head, Mom had to carry him in both hands.

"Bedtime, everyone!" Salazar called out. "Settle in, and I'll get you ready. You all know the routine."

In their curtained-off rooms, the patients climbed into their beds. They all stayed on their backs on top of the covers.

Salazar gave them time to get into place. "What grade are you in, Richard?" he asked.

"Sixth," I said.

"And are you interested in anything particular? Think you might like to be a doctor like your mom?"

7

I shrugged. "I don't really know," I muttered.

I hate it when people ask me what I want to be. I know Salazar was just trying to be nice. But I never know what to say. I mean, I'm only a kid. How do I know what I want to do with the rest of my life?

"You brought that old ventriloquist dummy," he said. "Are you interested in puppets?"

"Not really," I said.

He nodded. "Well, follow me. We'll start with Mr. Baldwin." He led the way to the first bed.

Mr. Baldwin was an older guy with a fringe of white hair around his head and a short white beard that covered most of his face. He wore a black night-shirt and black socks.

He squinted at me. "Are you Salazar's new assistant?"

Salazar answered for me. "It's Bring-Your-Kid-to-Work Day at the hospital," he said. "Richard has never seen what his mother does."

"She watches us sleep all night," Mr. Baldwin said. "I don't know how *she* manages to stay awake!"

"Are you feeling sleepy tonight, Mr. Baldwin?"

He groaned. "I feel tired all the time," he said. "Except at bedtime."

"We'll see how you do tonight," Salazar told him. He lifted a bunch of wires from the computer table beside the bed. "These are electrodes, Richard. We attach them to Mr. Baldwin, and they transmit his sleep patterns to the little monitors beside each bed— and to the big monitors in your mother's office."

He dipped an electrode into a gooey liquid and stuck it onto one side of Mr. Baldwin's forehead.

Then he attached a second electrode to the other side of his forehead.

"There are eight electrodes in all," Salazar explained to me.

"Did you ever see the movie *Frankenstein*?" Mr. Baldwin asked me. "That's what this looks like. It's what they did to the Frankenstein monster."

Salazar attached a few more electrodes. "There isn't anything scary about it," he said. "It allows us to see how deep Mr. Baldwin's sleep is, when he wakes up, when he dreams, anything that interrupts his sleep."

"Can you see his dreams?" I asked.

Salazar shook his head. "No. Only *when* he dreams, not *what* he dreams."

He hooked up the eighth electrode. "Pleasant dreams," he said. "I'll turn off all the lights when I get everyone online."

I followed him into the next curtained bedroom. Salazar talked quietly with all the patients as he attached the electrodes to them. Some of them appeared sleepy, but some seemed wide awake.

I wondered if I could fall asleep with all those wires connected to my skin. That might be hard. And I wondered how my mom stayed awake all night, watching the sleep patterns of six patients.

Salazar hooked up the last patient and pointed to the back room. "You can go see your mom now, Richard," he said. "She'll show you what she watches on the computer monitors."

I nodded and started toward the office. And on the way, I had an idea.

It was a funny idea. "Mom, I want to try hooking electrodes to someone," I said.

Mom laughed. "Why? Did that look like fun to you? It isn't as easy as it seems. They have to go in exactly the right place."

"I just want to try," I said. I picked up Slappy. "Can I try it on him? Can I hook up Slappy?"

She squinted at me. "Seriously?"

I nodded. "Come on. Let me try."

"Okay," she said. "Why not? Follow me."

I slung Slappy over my shoulder and followed Mom to one of the empty beds. "Put him down here on his back," she said.

I settled him on the bed. His eyes stayed closed, as if he was already asleep.

Mom arranged the wires and electrodes on the table beside the bed. She opened a tube of the gooey stuff and poured it into a small bowl. "Okay, go ahead," she said. "Dip the electrode into the gel and attach it to Slappy."

I did it just the way I had watched Salazar work. I stuck a wire on each side of Slappy's forehead. Then two on his neck. Three on his chest. And one on top of his head.

"Okay. Good job," Mom said. She turned and fiddled with the computer monitor on the table. "Let's see what we've got."

We both gazed at the screen as it came to life.

Suddenly, Mom's eyes went wide and she let out a loud gasp. "Whaaaat!" she cried. "I don't *believe* it!"

10

"Mom—what's wrong?" I cried.

She blinked several times and then squinted at the wiggly yellow lines going across the monitor.

"This . . . this doesn't make any sense!" Mom said. "I'm seeing *brain activity*. But that's *impossible*! That can't happen with a lifeless dummy."

Mom stared at the monitor. I heard a loud blip, and then a crackling sound. Like an electric shock.

The jagged yellow lines rolled across the screen. She gazed down at Slappy again. "Impossible," she murmured.

"I . . . I don't understand," I stammered. "Why are you upset?"

"Because a wooden dummy can't send out brain signals," she answered. "Look at the lines on the screen. You have to be *alive* to send out those brain waves."

I laughed. "Remember that cartoon movie we watched a few weeks ago? *Pinocchio*? Maybe Slappy is a real boy."

"And maybe I'm Mother Goose!" Mom shot back. She grabbed the wires I had connected to Slappy and ripped them all off with one hard tug.

11

The lines on the screen stopped jumping up and down and went totally flat.

"I know what's wrong," she said, setting the wires back on the table. "It has to be my equipment. There's definitely something wrong with the software or the connection."

She poked her head out into the hall. "Salazar?" she called in a loud whisper. She didn't want to wake her patients. "Are you there? I need you to reboot this unit and check the electrodes."

I picked up Slappy and followed Mom to her office. She checked the wall of monitors to see how her patients were doing. "These monitors seem to be working fine," she said.

Mom's cell phone rang. She glanced at its screen. "That's your dad. He's in the parking lot to take you home."

I groaned. "I thought I was staying all night with you," I said.

"No way, Richard. Tomorrow is school. And this is going to be a busy week. Don't forget about Willow."

My mouth dropped open. "Huh? Willow?"

Mom shook her head. "I thought I told you. She's coming to stay with us for a few days. Her parents are going on a business trip."

I couldn't keep the surprise off my face.

Mom narrowed her eyes at me. "You don't have a problem with that, do you?" she asked.

"Of course not," I answered.

Of *course* I had a problem with that.

The problem was WILLOW!

Willow and I are first cousins. She is twelve, like me, and she and my aunt and uncle live about half a mile away. She's in my science class at school.

Her parents travel all the time, and Willow always comes to stay with us. So we see each other a lot. Mom and Dad even call the guest room "Willow's room."

Willow and I don't really get along. I mean, we have nothing in common. We don't fight or anything. But we aren't alike at all. In fact, we are total opposites.

I am tall and dark and kind of serious-looking. Willow is short and has blond hair that bounces like a kitchen sponge. Her whole personality is bouncy like her hair.

Believe me, she's not shy like me. She laughs a lot and has a million friends and sometimes sings at the top of her lungs and isn't afraid of anything, as far as I can tell.

And she loves to play tricks on people.

I think she has a cruel sense of humor. But maybe that's because I would never *dream* of tricking anyone.

I guess my major problem with Willow is that she's always trying to get me to be more like her. She's always daring me to do things I don't want to do. Always trying to make me braver and bolder and less shy.

That can be seriously annoying.

After school the next afternoon, Willow and I were in the gym, at the back wall, working on our mural. Yes—somehow, we always end up working on projects together.

We had a huge sheet of paper taped to the wall, and a bunch of paint cans at our feet. Willow stood near the top of a ladder, painting an owl in a tree. I was on my knees below, working my brush up and down in short strokes, filling in the grass at the bottom of the painting.

"This is going to be awesome!" Willow gushed. "We need to work a lot more animals in."

"Careful!" I cried. "You're dripping paint on my head."

"Want to trade places with me?" she called down. "You can start on the sky."

"No thanks," I replied. "I don't like to be up on ladders."

We were painting the mural for our zoo overnight. Every year, the zoo sponsors an overnight sleepover for the Russet Middle School sixth-grade science class.

We get to have dinner in the Ape and Monkey House, and then a special up-close tour of the zoo animals. And then we have an all-night slumber party in sleeping bags.

14

It's a big deal. Willow and I wanted to do something special for it. It was her idea to paint a mural to put up at the zoo.

Willow climbed down and set her paint can on the floor. She had a strange grin on her face.

"Why are you smiling?" I asked.

Her grin grew wider. "I just did something funny," she said. She glanced all around, as if making sure no one could hear. But we were the only ones in the gym.

"Uh-oh," I murmured. "I don't think I want to know."

Willow leaned close to me. "Remember that ruler Mr. Trevino is always waving at us? The one he points at us with when he's unhappy about something?"

"Yes. I know the ruler," I said.

Mr. Trevino is the Art teacher, and he's always unhappy about *something*. And he swings that ruler and slaps his desk with it and threatens us with it all the time.

Willow lowered her voice to a whisper. "Well, just before I came here, I slopped blue paint all over the ruler and put it back in Trevino's drawer." She giggled. "When he reaches for it, he'll get blue paint smeared all over his hand."

I gasped. "But, Willow—he'll see us here with these paint cans. He'll know we had to be the ones who did it."

She shook her head. "No way. He went home for the day. He won't see us. And I put enough paint on the ruler so it will still be wet and sticky tomorrow morning." She laughed again at her own joke.

15

"I guess it's a *little* funny," I said.

Willow gave me a push toward the ladder. "Get up there and start the sky," she said.

"I told you, I don't like ladders," I said.

She shoved a paint can with a brush inside it into my hand. "This will be good for you, Richard. You can get over your fear. It's easy. Get up there." She gave me another push.

My heart started to pound as I climbed. The paint can swung in my right hand as I used my left hand to grip the ladder's side.

"You're doing great!" Willow called up to me. "See? It isn't scary at all."

I dipped the wide brush into the paint and raised it to the top of our mural. That's when I heard footsteps on the gym floor behind us.

I whipped my head around and saw Mr. Trevino striding toward us, taking long, heavy steps. He had one hand raised, and it had a thick blue stripe across the palm.

My legs started to collapse, and I nearly toppled off the ladder.

Trevino peered up at me. His face was red and angry. "Richard!" he boomed, his voice ringing off the gym walls. "I see you have blue paint up there!"

"I . . . uh . . ." I couldn't get any words out.

Trevino waved his blue hand in front of him. "Come down, Richard," he said. "We need to have a talk."

I slowly made my way down the ladder on shaky Jell-O legs.

Willow pressed her hands at her waist and stared

at me. "Richard—what did you *do*?" she cried. She could barely keep a straight face.

I wanted to dump the can of blue paint on her head. But, of course, I would never do anything like that.

"We can talk about this privately in the art room," Trevino said.

I set the blue paint can down and followed Mr. Trevino down the hall to my doom.

At dinner that night, Mom asked me how my day was. And I couldn't think of any good way to answer. "Willow and I worked on our mural," I said finally.

"Nice," Mom said.

No, it wasn't nice!

Thanks to Willow's little joke, Mr. Trevino said I had to come in after school for two weeks and clean the art room. It was totally unfair. But no way could I rat on Willow.

Willow was coming to stay with us the next night, and I desperately wanted to think up a way to pay her back.

I was still thinking about it when I went to bed.

And later . . . a short while later . . . I had my first terrifying dream.

5

I brushed my teeth and changed into my pajamas. I shudder every time I put these pajamas on. They are *Puppy Pal* pajamas, and I know that no one over the age of two would want to be caught dead in them. But Grandma Rose gave them to me for Christmas, and Mom and Dad made me keep them.

I carried Slappy to my bed and stretched him out at the foot. That's where he sleeps every night. That's not too weird, right? It made me feel calm knowing he was down there.

As I climbed into bed, I once again pictured Mom's startled expression as she stared at the monitor in her lab office. I pictured the jagged yellow lines rolling across the screen. And heard Mom's cries of alarm. "Impossible!" she shouted. "That's impossible!"

A smile crossed my face as I pulled the covers up to my chin. Mom's computer must have had some kind of bug. Slappy couldn't really have brain waves. But it sure gave Mom a shock.

A thought flashed into my mind. *Could I think up a way to use Slappy to scare Willow?*

I felt a cool breeze float against my face. The windows in my room are old, and the wind outside makes them rattle. Even when they are closed and locked, they let in a lot of cold air.

I was still thinking about Willow and Mr. Trevino's blue hand and all the trouble Willow's little joke got me into when I drifted off to sleep.

It was a restless sleep. I kept opening my eyes, half-awake, and rolling over from one side to the other. Finally, a deep darkness washed over me and I dropped into a comfortable snooze.

I don't know how long I slept. But I was jerked awake when I felt my covers tugged away. I gasped in the sudden cold air and sat straight up.

"Who—?" My voice was clogged from sleep.

My heart pounding, I squinted into the darkness—and saw two glowing eyes. A face. Up against mine.

Slappy.

"Huh?" I gasped again and felt a chill of fear run down my body.

The dummy stood on the floor beside the bed. He stood up straight, gripping my blankets in both wooden hands.

His grin shimmered darkly in the dim light from the window. His eyes stared, unblinking, into mine.

I tried to grab my covers back, but his grip was too tight. "Hey—" I choked out. I still couldn't speak.

"Richard!" he rasped my name in a hoarse voice. "Time to wake up, Richard."

"Uh . . . whoa," I murmured. "You *talk*?"

He uttered a shrill giggle. "I walk. I talk. I stalk."

"No. No way!" I cried. "You're a dummy. A wooden dummy. You can't—"

"Don't call me dummy, Dummy!" he shrieked. He shook the blankets angrily.

"Stop!" I cried. "I'm dreaming. I have to be dreaming."

"Snap out of it, dreamer," Slappy barked. "You have work to do."

"Work?" I uttered. "What kind of work?"

He giggled again. "Richard, your work is *whatever I say*!"

"I . . . I don't understand," I stammered. The cold air from the window seemed to swirl around me, and I shivered.

"You serve me now," Slappy rasped. "You will do everything I tell you."

"No. No way—" I said again.

"My servant *for life*!" Slappy screamed into my face.

I tried to pull away. But he dropped the blankets and grabbed my wrist. "Do I have to persuade you?" he cried.

"You can't persuade me," I said. "I'm not going to be your servant. Let go of me." My voice trembled, revealing my fear.

"We'll sssseee," he hissed.

Then he lowered his head, opened his mouth wide—and sank his wooden jaws into my arm.

"Owwwww." I let out a howl of pain. "Let go! Let go of me!"

I tugged and squirmed and struggled to pull free. But he held on tight. His head swung up and down with my frantic movements. And his hard mouth sank deeper into my skin, sending wave after wave of pain shooting through my arm and over my whole body.

"Let go! Let *go* of me! Please—stop! Let gooooo!"

I woke up screaming.

I was sitting straight up in bed. I struggled to catch my breath. I shivered under a cold sweat that drenched my forehead.

As I blinked myself awake, the room came into focus. Red morning sunlight washed in from the window.

My covers were still on the bed. And Slappy . . . Slappy still lay at the foot of the bed where I had left him.

"A dream," I murmured to myself "All a frightening dream." But it had seemed so real.

I turned and lowered my feet to the floor. I started to stand up, then stopped.

My arm. My arm ached.

I rolled up my pajama sleeve and examined it. Why was my arm red and sore?

Was it just from sleeping on it?

Mom picked Willow and me up after school that day. She tossed Willow's suitcase into the cargo area of our SUV. Willow and I climbed into the back seat.

Mom acted hurt. "No one wants to sit up front with me?"

"We want you to be our chauffeur," Willow said.

"Ooh. Big word," I said. "Are you trying to impress us?"

Willow pulled a wad of pink chewing gum from her mouth and stuck it on my nose.

I groaned. "Give me a break. Can you stop being so childish?"

"*I'm* the childish one?" Willow exclaimed. "I've seen you in your *Puppy Pal* pajamas!"

I could feel my face growing hot. Why did I always blush so easily?

"Richard," Mom called from the front seat, "why did you have to stay after school and clean the art room?"

"Uh . . . I'm doing it for extra credit," I said. That was pretty quick thinking for me. I usually just stammer and stutter and can't think of a good lie.

"Mr. Trevino likes Richard," Willow told my mom. "He thinks Richard has real painting talent." She grinned at me.

Not funny.

I punched her arm. Then she punched my arm. "Ow!" I cried out in pain, grabbing my arm. "Careful. My arm is sore."

Mom turned the car onto our block. "Sore? Sore from what?"

"I don't know," I said.

At home, Willow carried her suitcase to her room. "How long is she staying?" I asked my mom.

Mom frowned at me. "Be nice to her, Richard. Stop teasing her all the time."

"Huh? Me?"

"It must be hard on her to have her parents go away so often," Mom said.

No. It's hard on ME!

Willow came back and spotted my jigsaw puzzle on the table in the den. I followed her over to the table. "Hey, it's all black and white," she said.

"That's because it's panda bears," I said.

She squinted at it. "What do you do when it's finished? Mess it up and start again?" She spread a hand over it to mess it up.

I grabbed her arm away. "Stop!"

She laughed. "I wasn't really going to do it," she said.

"Sit down," I said. "You can help me. It's almost done. Help me finish it."

We pulled up chairs and began to work on the puzzle. There were only twelve or thirteen pieces left to put in.

23

Willow found a piece of a panda's eye and slid it into place. "It's so hard without any other colors," she said.

"They make puzzles that are all one color that are even harder," I said. "No picture or anything."

"Why would anyone do one of those?" Willow asked.

I shrugged. "Beats me."

I jumped up from the chair and cheered when I fit the last piece in. "Yaaaay. Done! Victory!" I cried.

Willow didn't celebrate with me. She pointed to the puzzle.

I glanced down and saw three holes in the puzzle. "Three pieces missing," I said. "Where are they?"

I searched the tabletop. Then I scooted my chair back and examined the carpet all around. No sign of them.

I groaned. "I don't believe it. I spent a week on this stupid puzzle, and I can't finish it because there are three pieces missing."

Willow tsk-tsked.

I banged both fists on the table. "It isn't fair. How could they sell me a puzzle with pieces missing?"

Willow's eyes flashed. A grin spread over her face. She opened her fist—and there were the three missing pieces.

"You—you—" I stammered.

"I just wanted to see what you would do," she said.

I reached both hands up to strangle her. But, of course, I didn't.

Dad walked into the room and set down his brief-case. "Hey, Willow. How's it going?" he said.

"Good. I'm just helping Richard with his jigsaw puzzle," she said.

Helping me?

"Well, it's dinnertime," Dad said. "Come sit down and tell us all your news."

We took our seats at the table. A platter of spaghetti and meatballs and a big salad bowl stood in the center. Willow sat across from me.

"You're sitting in Slappy's seat," I told her.

Willow rolled her eyes. "Do you really bring that dummy to the table?"

"Of course," I said. "Slappy likes to watch us eat."

Dad scooped a tall pile of spaghetti onto his plate. "We don't approve," he told Willow. "But we've given up. Richard brings that dummy everywhere."

"What's the big deal?" I snapped.

"Don't sound so angry," Mom said. "We're not making fun of you."

"Richard has been in a bad mood all day," Willow said, passing the salad bowl to Mom.

Mom peered at me. "How come, Richard?"

"Just tired, I think," I answered. "I didn't sleep much last night. I had a terrible nightmare."

"Can you share it?" Willow asked. "I love terrible nightmares. When they're someone else's!"

"Did you dream about my sleep lab?" Mom asked. "Is that what upset you?"

"Mom took me to her lab," I explained to Willow. "And these people were all hooked up to electrodes and sleeping on cots."

"Cool," Willow said. "Was it like a horror movie?"

"No," I said. "It wasn't scary at all. Mom was studying how they sleep to help them."

"So what was your nightmare about?" Dad asked, taking more spaghetti.

"Slappy," I said.

"No way," Mom said. "Now you're *dreaming* about him?"

"It was so real," I said. I felt a shiver roll down my back just thinking about it. "Slappy came to life— and he could talk. He pulled off my covers, and he said I had to be his servant and do whatever he told me for the rest of my life."

"That's seriously creepy," Willow murmured. She had her fork in the air. She had stopped eating to listen.

I nodded. "Yeah. Creepy," I said. "In the dream, I was terrified. But I told Slappy I wouldn't be his servant. And then . . . he bit me. I mean really hard. Sank his teeth into my arm. I screamed and screamed, and he wouldn't let go. It really hurt."

"And then what?" Willow asked.

"Then I woke up," I said. "I was covered in sweat and shaking all over. I looked down at the bottom of my bed, and Slappy was lying there, right where I left him. So I knew it was a dream. But . . . but . . ." My voice trailed off.

"But what?" Dad demanded.

"My arm was red and sore," I said. I rolled up my shirtsleeve. "Look. It's still red and sore."

They all squinted at the bruise on my arm. "Weird," Mom muttered.

"Know what I think?" Willow said. "I think when

26

you go to bed you should put that dummy in the closet."

"He always sleeps at the bottom of my bed," I said. "It was just a nightmare, Willow. No big deal."

"That's a good attitude," Dad said. "No big deal at all."

We all dug into our spaghetti and ate in silence for a while.

That night, I had another terrifying nightmare.

In the dream, I was wandering through an endless white light. The light was so bright, I had to shield my eyes with one hand.

Slowly, the brightness faded, and I saw long curtains on both sides of me. There were narrow beds between the curtains. I realized I was at my mom's sleep lab.

I heard people snoring and machines beeping all around. I couldn't see any of the patients. They all seemed to be totally hidden under white bedsheets.

I began to feel frightened. Where was my mom?

I strode through the hall, searching for her. I saw only curtains and beds . . . curtains and beds. No people. The beeping of the machines grew louder.

"Mom?" I called to her in a hoarse, troubled voice. "Mom?"

The curtains began to swirl around me, circling me. I felt myself being surrounded, pulled inside them.

And suddenly, the scene changed. I was in bed. On my back. Long white curtains closed me in. The bedsheet was pulled to my chin.

The sheet felt heavy. Like a weight pressing down on me. I tried to raise my arms, and I couldn't!

I started to struggle. I knew I had to get out of that bed. I squirmed one way, then the other. I tried to kick my legs. But I couldn't free myself.

Shaking in fear, I saw a flash of light before my eyes. My mom appeared beside the bed. She was in her white lab uniform. She gazed down at me.

"Mom—I'm so glad to see you!" I cried. "I couldn't find you anywhere. Can you get me out of this bed?"

She didn't answer. She stared at me a moment longer. Then she moved to the computer equipment on the other side of the bed and began pulling out wires.

"Mom? Are you going to help me?" My voice came out all shaky with fear.

Again, she didn't answer. She tugged at the wires. Then she raised an electrode over me and pressed it onto my forehead.

"Stop!" I cried. "Why are you doing this?"

She pressed another electrode onto my left cheek.

"Mom—I'm not a patient!" I cried, feeling the panic roll over me. "Stop! I don't want to do this. Let me up!"

She didn't answer. She tugged down the bedsheet and attached an electrode to my throat. Then she pressed one onto my left shoulder.

"Mom—"

She turned her back to me and fiddled with the monitor controls. I watched her pull out more electrodes.

"Mom, please—"

She turned around quickly. And as she spun toward me, I saw that it wasn't my mom anymore. *It was Slappy!*

29

Slappy in my mother's white lab coat. The dummy's eyes flashed in the bright lights, and his grin appeared to grow wider. He pushed an electrode onto my chest.

"Nooooo!" A long scream escaped my throat. "Slappy—please!" I choked out.

He tossed back his head and laughed. A crazy, cold laugh.

"Let me up! Let me out!" I screamed. Again, the heavy sheet kept me pressed to the bed.

"Pleasant dreams!" Slappy cried. He laughed again.

I watched him throw a switch at the side of the computer monitor.

And—*zzzzzzzaaaaaaaap!*

I shrieked as I felt a jolt of electricity shoot through my body. The powerful shock sent me flying up from the bed. The pain exploded in my head and down my chest.

I dropped back down, gasping for breath.

Zzzzzzzaaaaaapppppp.

I heard the buzz of the current before a second explosion of pain rocked my body.

Slappy kept his hand on the switch. His wide grin shimmered in my eyes.

"Please! It hurts!" I wailed. "I can't *stand* it!"

Zzzzzzzzzaaaaaaaapppppppp.

I sat up wide awake, breathing hard.

My hands and feet tingled. But I didn't feel any pain.

The dream stayed with me. I shook my head hard, trying to get the buzz of the electric shocks from my mind.

Another nightmare. So real, my whole body wouldn't stop trembling.

I sat up and took a few deep breaths.

The picture of Slappy grinning in his white lab coat refused to fade away.

I turned to the foot of the bed. The dummy lay on its side, just where I had left him. His eyes were closed, and his mouth hung open lifelessly.

I reached down and grabbed him around the waist and sat him up. "Slappy, why am I suddenly having nightmares about you?" I demanded. My voice was hoarse from sleep.

The dummy stared back at me, mouth still hanging open.

I didn't bother to get dressed. I ran to the kitchen in my pajamas. I had to tell my parents about this new nightmare. So real. So terrifying. I couldn't shake it.

I burst into the kitchen to find Willow already at the breakfast table, across from my mom. They turned when they heard me enter the room—and they both burst out laughing.

"Wh-what's so funny?" I stammered.

They both pointed.

"Your hair," Mom said. "It's sticking up in all directions. Like you've just been struck by lightning!"

"Huh?" I gasped.

"Did you stick your finger in an electrical socket?" Willow said. "I thought that only happens in cartoons!"

I grabbed the sides of my head with both hands and tried to smooth down my hair. But every time I pulled it down, it jumped right back up.

"I . . . had another nightmare," I said. "It was really bad."

"A nightmare about Slappy?" Willow asked.

I nodded. "Yeah. About Slappy."

"So did I!" Willow exclaimed.

I squinted at her. "You're joking," I murmured.

"No way!" she said. "I had a really frightening dream and Slappy was in it."

Mom took a long sip from her coffee mug. "Both of you? How is that possible?" she said. "That's quite a coincidence."

I sat down at the end of the table and poured myself a glass of orange juice from the pitcher. I studied Willow. "This is another one of your jokes, right? You're making fun of me?"

She raised her right hand. "No. I swear, Richard.

I had a nightmare about Slappy. I woke up scream-ing. Didn't you hear me?"

I reached for the Corn Flakes box. "Tell me your dream," I demanded. "Let's hear it, Willow. What was your nightmare about?"

"I was on the school bus," Willow started. "I was coming home from school. I think you were on the bus, too, Richard. But I'm not sure. I was sitting in a middle row, and I think you were in the back."

"Was the bus crowded?" I asked.

Willow shut her eyes, thinking. "No. It was empty. There were no other kids around me." She frowned at me. "Don't interrupt. Just let me tell it, okay?"

I shrugged and stirred the cereal in my bowl.

"I remember I was watching trees roll past the bus window," Willow continued. "Suddenly, the trees whizzed by faster. I realized the bus had picked up speed."

Willow spun her juice glass tensely between her hands. "The ride became very bumpy. I bounced up and down. Once or twice, I felt myself bouncing out of my seat.

"In the dream, I shut my eyes. I gritted my teeth. My hands were clasped so hard in my lap, they ached. Faster. The bus picked up more speed and began to zigzag from one side of the street to the other.

"I heard horns honking. I heard people shouting out in the street.

"I stared out the bus window as the bus rocketed past my house. It swung around a corner with such a deafening *squeal*, I had to cover my ears.

"I gripped the back of the seat in front of me and struggled to stay in my seat as the bus rocked harder. Then the brakes screeched and we just missed ramming into a car. I was thrown hard against the window. I thought we were going to turn over!

"Finally, I found my voice. I opened my mouth and started to scream. It was so real. I didn't know I was dreaming. I thought it was really happening.

"'Stop! Please STOP!' I wailed. 'Stop the bus! I want off! STOP!'

"The bus stopped with a hard bump. I was thrown to my feet. I stumbled into the aisle. I was screaming at the driver. 'Let me OFF! Let me OFF!'

"I could only see the back of his head. I heard a cold, shrill laugh. And then slowly, the driver turned around to face me. *And it was Slappy!*

"Slappy, laughing his head off, his eyes rolling in his head. He gripped the wheel with both hands and bounced up and down in the driver's seat, laughing and cackling.

"I stood there in the aisle, staring at him in shock. And then he turned his head back to the windshield and started to drive again. The bus roared as it picked up speed.

"And then everything went crazy. The bus jolted hard.

"A deafening *crasssshhh* sent me stumbling down the aisle. I fell to my knees.

"I screamed in fright. I pulled myself to my feet. And now Slappy stood in front of me. He stared hard at me, and his evil grin grew wider.

"He raised both hands high. And the bus began to break apart. The seats flew to pieces. The windows all shattered. Everything around me broke apart, pieces flying everywhere. Like a jigsaw puzzle being ripped apart. And Slappy waved his hands again, and I went flying. I flew right out of the bus, into the sky, screaming all the way.

"I woke up screaming," Willow finished.

"Whoa," Mom said, her coffee mug in midair. She hadn't taken a sip. She had been listening to Willow's dream so intently. "What a frightening dream, Willow. And you remembered every single detail of it."

Willow shuddered. "I can't force it from my mind."

"My dream was scary, too," I said. I told them about being in the sleep lab and Slappy shocking me with electrodes.

"I guess you *did* find your visit to my lab disturbing," Mom said.

"But that doesn't explain why Willow and I both dreamed about Slappy," I replied.

"I still think you should put that dummy in a closet at night," Willow said.

I shook my head. "How will that keep him out of our dreams?" I asked her.

"We can talk about this tonight," Mom said. "Maybe your dad will have some ideas." She motioned

36

for us to stand. "Better hurry. You'll be late for school."

I raised the cereal bowl to my mouth and slurped down the rest of the milk. Then I climbed to my feet and began to walk to my room.

But I stopped at the door to the den—and froze.

"Oh, wow," I murmured, gazing into the room.

My jigsaw puzzle. It had been ripped apart. Pieces were scattered over the table, on the couch, all over the carpet.

"Willow!" I screamed. "Did you *do* this?"

She ran up beside me. "Do what?" Then she saw the destroyed puzzle. "Noooo," she murmured. "No. I didn't do that. I swear."

We both stared at the mess. Pieces everywhere.

"Just like the bus. Just like in my dream," Willow whispered.

SLAPPY HERE, EVERYONE.

Hahahaha.

Poor Richard. After all that hard work. Who would do a thing like that to his puzzle? Just thinking about it makes me go to pieces! (With laughter, that is.)

Speaking of dreams, lots of people describe me as *dreamy*. Wouldn't you like me to be *your* dream date? Hahaha.

I'll tell you one thing for sure about Richard and Willow—from now on, their dreams won't exactly be a yawn!

Something strange was going on.

I guess that was pretty obvious.

Mom drove Willow and me to school. Willow sat beside her up front, and I was in the back seat. Outside the car window, gray wisps of fog swirled up from the ground. Dark clouds hung low overhead, making it almost as dark as night.

It fit my mood perfectly.

"We never get fog like this," Mom said. "My fog lights are barely cutting through it."

"How did my puzzle get messed up?" I muttered. I wasn't really talking to them. I was talking to myself.

Mom shook her head but didn't say anything.

"I know you think I did it," Willow said. "But I didn't."

"Maybe your dad bumped the table when he was heading out to work," Mom said. "He got up very early this morning and it was totally dark."

"Bumped the table?" I said. "And the pieces flew all over the room? I don't think so, Mom."

"Richard, your nightmares are easy to explain," Mom said. "Your visit to my sleep lab was troubling to you. It upset you without you realizing it." She turned the corner onto the school block. "That's why you dreamed about the sleep lab last night. And that's why you've been having nightmares."

"It doesn't explain why Willow also had a nightmare last night," I said. "And it doesn't explain why Willow dreamed about Slappy, too."

"That dummy would give *anyone* nightmares," Willow said. "I really think you should get rid of it."

"Get rid of it?" I cried. "No way! That was my birthday present! Also—Slappy is my friend."

"Friend? Are you *kidding* me?" Willow tossed her head back and laughed.

"Enough talk," Mom said. "Get out, you two. We're here."

I climbed out of the car and swung my backpack over my shoulder. Willow trotted up the walkway toward the school entrance.

"Richard?" Mom called from the car. "Wake up. Stop yawning and yawning!"

"Did you forget? I haven't had any sleep in two nights!" I called back.

She sighed and shook her head. I watched her drive off.

Then I followed Willow into the school.

We were late. The hall was nearly empty. Some of the classroom doors were already closed.

I hung my coat in my locker and hurried to Miss Deaver's classroom.

Willow was already at her table near the front. I started toward my place near the window. And felt a wave of hot air surround me.

"Take your seat, Richard," Miss Deaver said. She was fanning herself with a magazine. "We've already been talking about the heat in here."

Miss Deaver is young, with straight black hair she twists in a single braid, dark eyes, and a nice smile. She wears faded jeans and brightly colored sweaters to school every day.

She speaks very softly and sometimes it's hard to hear her. I think she's so quiet because she's secretly shy, like me. But I don't know if that's true.

"The school boiler has gone berserk," Miss Deaver told me. "The heat is unbearable. It must be one hundred degrees in here."

"Can we go home and get our bathing suits?" Brandy Linker asked.

Some kids laughed.

Brandy sits next to me, and she isn't shy at all. She's always shouting out her comments, and actually, she's pretty funny.

"Well, we can pretend we're at the beach," Miss Deaver replied. "What a shame the classroom windows don't open. But the custodian is working on the heat. It shouldn't be this hot for long."

I yawned. The heat was making me even sleepier. My eyes started to close. I forced myself to sit up straight and be alert.

"Biology today," Miss Deaver said. She pointed to two girls at the front table. "Help me pass out the jars."

I tried to hold in another yawn.

"We are going to continue with our frog dissections," Miss Deaver said. "So everybody sit next to your lab partner."

I already sat next to my lab partner. It was Brandy. In the first session, she was a lot bolder than me. I mainly watched while she did the cutting.

"One of your parents complained that the dissections were cruel to frogs," Miss Deaver said. "So I want to assure you that no frogs died in the making of this science lesson. These frogs all died of natural causes."

Brandy leaned close to me. "They probably all had heart attacks when they heard they were going to be cut up," she said.

I laughed.

Miss Deaver went around the room, dropping X-Acto knives in front of us. They have narrow metal blades and are seriously sharp.

Our frog was delivered in its formaldehyde jar. Brandy lifted it out carefully and placed it on the table.

I wiped sweat off my forehead with my shirtsleeve. The heat seemed to be going up, not cooling off. The bitter smell of the formaldehyde invaded my nose, and I started to choke.

Brandy put the lid back on and shoved the jar away from us.

I yawned again. The heat was making me feel so drowsy. I felt my head sinking forward.

Brandy grabbed my shoulder and shook me. "Richard, are you *fainting*?" she demanded.

I snapped alert. "No. Just sleepy," I said. "It's ... so hot in here ... and I didn't sleep much last night ... and ..."

At the front of the room, Miss Deaver started to give instructions. "You all got off to a good start last time," she said. I didn't hear the next thing she said. She was speaking so softly.

I gazed at the frog on its back on the table in front of us. And struggled to hear Miss Deaver's words ... struggled to concentrate.

But suddenly, the room went dark. I felt hands over my eyes. Hands covering my eyes.

"Guess who?" a shrill voice demanded.

"Huh? Who?" I gasped.

The hands slid away from my face. I spun around. And stared at Slappy standing behind me.

"Did you miss me?" he cried.

11

"You can't be here!" I said.

The dummy grinned at me. He brought his face close to mine. "Well, I'm here!" he rasped. He opened his mouth wide and cackled.

"No. No way," I said. "You can't talk. And you can't be in school."

He cackled again. "Who makes the rules?" he said in his shrill voice.

I started to stand up. But he raised both wooden hands and pushed me back into my chair.

"Richard—what's happening?" Brandy cried. She had the X-Acto knife in her hand. "Sit down. Pay attention. What's *wrong* with you?"

"I—I can't," I stammered. "Slappy—he's here. I have to deal with him."

The dummy laughed again. "Go ahead. Deal with me!" he said. "You can *try*!"

"You can't follow me to school," I said, my voice cracking. "You have to leave. You can't be here on your own."

"I'm not on my own," Slappy replied. His green

eyes shut, then opened again. "You are here, Richard. You are my lab partner."

"N-no!" I stuttered. "No way. Brandy is my lab partner. You are just a dummy. You can't be here!"

"Don't call me dummy, Dummy!" he screeched.

"What is happening? Richard? What is happening?" Brandy repeated.

Didn't she see Slappy standing beside me?

I glanced around the room. Everyone was bent over their frog dissections. No one saw the dummy.

"Be a good servant," Slappy said. "You won't be happy if you disobey me, Richard."

"I'm not your servant! I'm *not!*" I screamed.

"Be a good lab partner," Slappy said. He waved his hand over the table. "Pick up the frog."

"No," I said. "I won't. You have to go away."

"What is happening? What is happening?" Brandy kept repeating those words over and over.

Slappy raised a hand and pressed it against my neck. "Owww!" I let out a cry as he tightened his fingers. He squeezed my neck until pain shot down my whole side.

"L-let go. Please—" I begged. "You—you're *hurting* me!"

"Pick up the frog," he rasped in my ear. "I don't like to hurt you, partner, but I can!"

"Okay, okay. Just let go of my neck," I said.

I felt his hand loosen. I picked up the frog by its two back legs.

"That's better, Richard," Slappy said. "You are catching on."

My whole body was shivering. "What should I do with the frog?" I asked.

"Eat it," Slappy rasped.

"No. Really," I said. I dangled the frog in front of me. "What do you want me to do with the frog?"

Slappy pressed his wooden face close to mine. "You are going to eat it," he whispered. "Go ahead. Prove your loyalty to me."

"M-my loyalty?" I stammered.

"Eat the frog!" he shouted into my ear, so loud I flinched.

"No. I—"

"Eat it! Eat the frog! Eat it! Eat it! Eat it!"

I felt my stomach lurch. I started to gag. I swung the frog upside down in front of me.

"Eat it! Eat it! *Eat it!*"

I blinked. I opened my eyes wide. Slappy disappeared.

I turned to Brandy. She wasn't there, either.

I heard voices. The other kids in the class had turned to stare at me.

I saw Brandy standing beside Miss Deaver at the front of the class.

"Richard, are you okay?" Miss Deaver came walking toward me. "Brandy came up here to tell me you had fallen asleep."

"I tried to wake you, but I couldn't," Brandy said.

"I . . . I guess I'm okay," I stammered. "It was so hot in here . . . and I didn't sleep last night . . ."

Miss Deaver peered down at the table in front of me. "Richard? Where is your frog?" she asked.

"Excuse me?"

"Your frog," the teacher repeated. "I don't see it here."

I suddenly realized I had a sick, burning taste in my mouth.

"Oh nooooo," I moaned.

"Richard, what's wrong?" the teacher asked.

"I think I ate it."

12

"And then what happened?" Dad asked.

"We found the frog on the floor under the table," I said.

"So you didn't swallow any formaldehyde?" Willow asked.

"Enough," Mom said. "Change the subject. You're making me sick."

We were finishing our dinner. Dad had brought home fish and chips from the restaurant across from his store. Mom had made a big pot of canned New England clam chowder to go with it.

We had talked about my Slappy dream and the dead frog through the whole meal. Willow and Dad didn't want to talk about anything else.

Willow studied me from across the table. "Formaldehyde is poison, isn't it?" she asked.

"Probably," Dad answered. "It *can't* be good for you."

"Are you okay, Richard?" Mom asked. "You hardly touched your fish and chips."

"Yes I did," I said. "I had two pieces. I feel okay. It's just that . . ."

"Just that what?" Dad asked.

I scraped my fork back and forth across my dinner plate. I felt so tense, like a spring inside me was wound up tight. "What am I going to do?" I said. "Every time I fall asleep, I see Slappy."

Mom bit her bottom lip. "It *is* very weird," she murmured.

"Every time I close my eyes, there he is," I said. "And he's always scary. The dreams are all frightening. He . . . he keeps saying I'm his servant. And then things go out of control, and it's all terrifying."

"I'm afraid to go to sleep in this house," Willow chimed in. "I mean, I *hate* nightmares!"

"It's not about you, Willow," I snapped.

"Let's not fight about who is the most scared," Mom said.

"There are plenty of nightmares to go around," Dad said. He chuckled.

I scowled at him. "Dad, was that supposed to be a joke?"

Mom shook her head. "The odd thing is, it all started after your visit to my sleep lab. I can't imagine why—"

"I wasn't freaked out about the lab," I told her. "It didn't scare me at all. I knew those patients were there to get help. I thought it was interesting—but not scary."

"Then how do you explain it?" Mom said.

We sat there in a heavy silence for a while.

"I know one thing," Willow said finally. "You should lock that dummy in a closet somewhere. Don't keep him on your bed."

"Maybe . . . ," I started.

"He's there at the foot of your bed," Willow said. "That means he's the last thing you see before you fall asleep."

"But he's just a doll," I argued. "A wooden dummy. What difference does it make where I put him?"

"Willow might be right," Dad said. "It's worth a try, Richard."

"Yes," Mom agreed. "If he's out of sight, maybe he'll be out of mind, too."

I sighed. "Okay. I'll stash him in the back of my closet before I go to bed."

"And maybe we'll *both* get some sleep," Willow said.

Mom passed out chocolate chip cookies for dessert. I carried mine to my bedroom. I had a research paper to write for English class. I felt so weary, my eyelids kept drooping. I hoped I could stay awake to write it, or at least get it started.

Slappy lay sprawled on his back on the bed, just where I had left him this morning. His eyes were wide open, gazing blankly at the ceiling. His mouth hung open in his usual grin.

"You're a troublemaker," I told him. "But I'm going to deal with you later."

I took a few bites of the cookie, then sat down at my laptop. I had a pile of notes I had printed out, and I pulled them beside the computer.

Since my science class was going to have that overnight at the zoo, I decided to write my research paper on the history of zoos. It was pretty interesting. Back in the 1700s, zoos started out as private animal collections.

50

Rich people bought animals from all over the world and kept them in their backyards. The richer you were, the more animals you could keep. They called them *zoological gardens*. And they were just for the entertainment of the owners.

It wasn't until many years later that the animal collections were opened up to the public. The first zoo in the U.S. was the Philadelphia Zoo. It opened in 1874.

I had printed out a lot of great info about zoos. Now I just had to write an introduction and put it all in a good order.

I leaned over the keyboard and began to write. The letters kept blurring in front of my eyes. But I forced myself to concentrate.

I wanted to write at least half of the essay tonight. Tomorrow was Saturday, and I didn't want to spend the whole weekend working on it.

I forced myself to keep typing. I wrote about a few of the big estates in France and the different animals people kept on them.

My fingers fumbled over the keys. I sighed. *I'm too tired,* I told myself. *I'll do more tomorrow.*

I stood up and stretched. Yawning, I pulled my pajamas from the top dresser drawer. I tossed my clothes on the floor and tugged on the pajamas.

"Okay, Slappy," I said. "No bedtime here for you tonight. Time for you to hit the closet."

I walked over to the bed.

Slappy was gone.

13

"No way!" I muttered.

I stared at the bed. The bedspread was smooth and empty.

Did the dummy fall off the bed? I checked the floor on both sides. No sign of him. I dropped onto my knees and searched under the bed. No Slappy.

"This is ridiculous," I whispered, climbing to my feet.

I jumped when I felt a tap on my shoulder. "*You're* ridiculous!" a shrill voice rasped.

Gasping, I spun around. And stared in shock at Slappy.

He stood straight up, his green eyes peering into mine, his grin glowing under the ceiling light. His wooden hand tapped my shoulder again.

"Time to get a move on, Richard," he said. He bounced up and down as he spoke.

"This isn't happening," I said.

"Did you forget you have a job to do, *servant*?" he cried.

"J-job?" I stuttered.

He nodded. "To do whatever I tell you to do!" he rasped. "Get dressed. Stop stalling."

"Get dressed?" I said. "Where are we going? I can't go out. It's late at night."

"Never too late to go to school," he replied. He motioned to the pile of my clothes on the floor. "Hurry, Richard. I don't want to hurt you. But I *can*! Hahaha."

"W-we can't go to school in the middle of the night," I stammered.

His grin appeared to grow wider. "Haven't you ever heard of *night* school?" He laughed again, that shrill, cold laugh. I guess he thought that was a joke.

The house was dark. Everyone had gone to bed.

I followed Slappy out the front door. We stepped into a clear, cool night. A tiny sliver of a moon floated high in the sky. It was silent outside, a deep silence I had never heard before.

The only sound was the pounding of my heart. Questions swirled round and round in my brain. *Why are we going to my school? What does Slappy want me to do? How can I escape from him?*

My school is an old-fashioned brick building, two stories tall. A few dim lights glowed in some of the downstairs classroom windows. There were no cars in the parking lot. No one in sight.

"We'll go around the back," Slappy said. "We can find a window to climb in."

"Wh-what if we're caught?" I stammered.

"Good question," he answered.

"Why are we here?" I demanded. "What am I supposed to do here?"

"You have work to do," he said, his shrill voice ringing in the silent air.

53

He led the way across the grass to an open window at the back of the school. "In you go, Richard," he whispered.

I crossed my arms in front of my chest. "What if I refuse?" I said.

His green eyes flashed in the pale moonlight. "Do you like your face? Do you want to keep it?" He grabbed my nose, tightened his fingers around it, and twisted it hard. "How about a nose job? Hahahaha!"

I let out a howl of pain. "Okay, okay," I muttered. I hoisted myself onto the windowsill and lowered myself into the school.

Slappy scrambled in after me. We were in the music room. The piano stood out darkly in the silvery light from the window. I took a deep breath and held it, trying to slow my racing heartbeats.

Was anyone else in the school? The cleaning staff? Was I about to be caught?

"Wh-where are we going?" I asked in a trembling whisper.

The dummy gave me a hard shove with both hands. "To the gym, of course."

I made my way down the hall on rubbery legs. A few dim ceiling bulbs cast small circles of light on the floor. I pushed open the double doors to the gym.

Total darkness.

I kept blinking, waiting for my eyes to adjust. Pale light washed in from a row of tiny windows high above. My footsteps tapped loudly in the huge room.

Slappy led the way to the far end. In the shadows, I could make out the mural Willow and I had started. The paper stretched across the back gym wall.

"Start painting," Slappy ordered. "Pick up that brush. Open the paint can. Start painting."

"Paint? I can't," I said. "It's too dark. I can't see a thing."

"Start painting," he repeated. He bent down and picked a gallon paint can up from the floor. "Paint, Richard." He waved the paint can in front of me.

"Why?" I demanded. "What do you want me to paint?"

"My face," the dummy rasped. "Paint my face on the mural."

"I can't," I told him. "Listen to me, Slappy. It's too dark."

"But my face *lights up* any painting!" he cried.

"I don't want to get in trouble. I can't do it," I said.

"You've *got* trouble!" he screamed. "When you refuse to obey me, you've *got* trouble."

Before I could move, he pulled the paint can backward—then swung it forward.

I cried out as a wave of dark paint rushed over me. I raised my hands—too late. The thick paint splashed over my head and oozed down my face, my shoulders . . . my body.

"Nooooo." I raised both hands and tried to wipe the paint away from my eyes. But another heavy splash knocked me back against the wall. Another wave of paint roared over me.

Struggling to wipe it away from my face, I saw Slappy raise another big can. "Nooooo!" I screamed again as more paint washed over me.

"I . . . can't . . . breathe!" I gasped. "Choking me . . . choking me . . . Please . . . stop! I can't breathe!"

14

"Choking . . . I'm choking . . ."

Slappy shook my shoulders.

I turned around.

No. Not Slappy. I gazed up at Willow, standing behind me.

"The paint," I said. "I'm drenched. I—"

"You were having a nightmare," Willow said. "You were muttering to yourself, Richard. Having a nightmare."

I checked myself out. No paint. I wasn't covered in paint. And I wasn't in school. I sat at my desk, my laptop dark in front of me.

Willow squinted at me, studying me. She was in a long yellow nightshirt, and her hair was wild around her face. "You okay?" she asked quietly.

I nodded. "I guess. I was writing my essay, and I must have fallen asleep here at my desk."

I raised my eyes to the bed. Slappy lay there on his back, eyes wide open. The dummy hadn't moved.

"I had another bad dream about Slappy," I told Willow.

"So did I!" she cried. "That's why I came to your room. To tell you."

I swept a hand back through my hair. My forehead was drenched in sweat. "You had another nightmare?"

She nodded. "It was horrible. Slappy made me go to school. To the gym."

"Me too!" I cried.

"He made me paint his face on our mural," Willow said. "He said I had to paint whatever he told me because I was his servant. And I would be his servant forever."

"We . . . we almost had the exact same dream!" I said. I jumped to my feet. "But . . . how is that possible?"

Willow shrugged. We both stared at the dummy, sprawled lifelessly on his back.

"As soon as I fall asleep, there he is," I said. "It's like he's there waiting. Waiting to invade my dreams."

I shivered. This was just too frightening to think about.

"It can't be an accident," Willow said. "It can't be a coincidence."

I sighed. "What are we going to do?" I said.

Willow walked over to my bed. "The first thing we're going to do," she said, "is stuff this dummy away in the closet."

She lifted Slappy off the bed. His head fell back, and his arms and legs dangled toward the floor. "He's heavier than I thought," Willow said.

She struggled to hold him right-side up. But his

58

body tilted to one side in her arms. "Hey—!" I cried out as a slip of paper fell out of his jacket pocket. "What's that?"

Willow set the dummy back down on the bed. "Check it out, Richard."

I picked the piece of paper off the rug and unfolded it. My eyes scanned the strange words printed on the page in red ink. "It says: *Don't read these words aloud unless you want to bring Slappy to life.*"

I squinted at the page. "Then there's a bunch of funny words."

"What words?" Willow strode up behind me and peered over my shoulder at the paper.

"*Karru Marri Odonna Loma Molonu Karrano,*" I read.

"Oh, wow." Willow slapped my shoulder gently. "Richard— do you realize what you just did?" she cried. "You just brought the dummy to life!"

I laughed. "Oh, for sure," I said. "Who would ever believe a story like that?"

15

We both turned to the bed. Slappy lay there on his side, where Willow had dropped him. "Do you really expect him to get up and do a dance?" I said.

Willow shrugged. "Why would someone put those words in his pocket if it wasn't true?" she demanded.

"As a joke?" I said. "You've heard of jokes, haven't you?"

Willow stared hard at the dummy. "He's already alive . . . in our dreams," she said. She turned to me, and I could see she was really frightened. "What if it's true, Richard? What if he's some kind of evil thing, and we just brought him to life?"

She stared hard at the dummy, her hands clasped into tense fists. "What if we woke him up? He was asleep, so he could only torture us in our dreams. But if he's awake now, what will he do to us?"

I didn't want to believe it. I didn't even want to think about it. I folded up the paper in my hand. I crossed the room and stuffed it back into Slappy's jacket pocket.

"This isn't a horror movie, Willow," I said. "This is real life." I lifted one of the dummy's arms, then let it fall lifelessly to the bed. "Look at him. Does he look alive to you?"

"He looked *very* alive in my dream," Willow replied. "And you woke up choking because of him."

"Dreams are different," I said. I grabbed Slappy under his arms and lifted him off the bed. "Open the closet door. I still think we should put him in there so maybe we won't dream about him."

Willow pulled open the door to my clothes closet. It's a long, narrow closet with shelves down one side. I carried Slappy to the back of the closet. I set him on a shelf, and then I buried him under two folded-up blankets.

"That should hold him," I told Willow, stepping into the room.

Willow frowned. "Does the closet door lock?"

"No," I said. "But I piled blankets on top of him." I closed the closet door and made sure it clicked shut. "He isn't going to move," I told Willow. "Stop thinking he could be alive. I only did this to maybe keep him out of our dreams."

Willow sighed. "I'll never get to sleep. I know I'll be up all night."

"Just don't think about Slappy," I said. "I'm going to concentrate on our class sleepover at the zoo. I'm going to shut Slappy from my mind."

"Good luck," Willow said. She disappeared into the hall. A few seconds later, I heard her close the door to her room.

Yawning, I changed into my pajamas. I took one last glance at the closet door before I clicked off the light. Then I climbed into bed and pulled the covers up to my chin.

I shut my eyes and tried to picture zoo animals. But Slappy's face kept flashing in my mind. Willow was right. It was going to be difficult to fall asleep.

I didn't want another Slappy nightmare. They were too frightening and too real.

I lay there for what must have been hours, gazing up at the shifting shadows on the ceiling made by the moonlight outside my window.

Finally, my eyelids drooped, as heavy as if they weighed a thousand pounds. I could feel myself drifting off to sleep.

THUD.

My eyes flew open at the strong bump.

Where did it come from? The closet?

I listened hard. Fully awake again.

I heard another *thud.*

"Noooo," I whispered. I sat up and held my breath.

I heard a soft scraping sound. Another thud. Definitely from the closet.

He isn't alive, I told myself. *That can't happen. He isn't alive,* I repeated.

I lowered my feet to the floor. I hugged myself to stop my sudden trembling. I concentrated so hard, I had a whistling in my ears, as if I could hear the *air!*

I stood, twisting free of the tangled bedsheets. I blinked in the darkness. I couldn't see a thing. The entire room was blanketed in deep shadow.

Another soft scraping noise. From the closet.

I've GOT to be imagining this! He isn't alive. He isn't alive.

I took a step toward the closet. My heartbeat began to race. I suddenly felt a chill prickling my entire body.

Another step.

I realized I was holding my breath. I let the air out in a long whoosh.

I stopped at the closet door. And listened. My hand felt cold and clammy against the metal doorknob.

Go ahead, I told myself.

I turned the knob and pulled the closet door open. Then I clicked on the closet light—and gasped.

16

I squinted into the bright light of the closet. I gazed down the row of shelves along the wall.

Nothing moved. Nothing moving.

My old pair of sneakers was lined up next to my snow boots. A stack of old graphic novels stood on the floor beside them. Nothing had changed.

I crept to the back of the closet. I peered at the two folded-up blankets I had piled on top of Slappy. They hadn't moved.

I began to breathe normally. *It's weird what your imagination can do to you*, I told myself.

Those bumps and scrapes—they *had* to be my imagination.

I needed to sleep. I was obviously overtired. Like Dad always says, I needed to recharge my brain cells.

I let out a long sigh of relief. Then I clicked off the closet light and shut the door behind me.

I was shivering when I climbed back under the covers. My room is the coldest room in the house. The windows leak. For some reason, my radiator makes a lot of banging and groaning. But it doesn't throw off much heat.

I'll bet that's what I was hearing, I told myself. *I was hearing the banging from the radiator.*

Feeling better, I shut my eyes and tried to fall asleep.

I pictured zoo animals passing by me, one by one. But that didn't make me feel sleepy. So I tried picturing the faces of the kids in my science class. I started with the kids at the front table, and I went around the table, picturing each kid.

I knew I was very tired. But I could not get to sleep. I had gone around the class twice before I finally felt my eyelids begin to grow heavy.

I glanced at the clock on my bedtable. It was a little after five in the morning. I'd been up almost the whole night. Outside my window, the sky was brightening from black to purple. The sun would be coming up soon.

I yawned and shifted onto my side.

Sleep, Richard . . . , I urged myself. *Go to sleep . . .*

Finally, I must have fallen asleep. Darkness washed over me. I didn't dream. A deep, silent sleep.

The red morning sun through my window woke me up. I groaned, sat up, and stretched my hands above my head. I rubbed my eyes, trying to force the sleep away.

"Morning already," I muttered to myself.

I squinted across the room. My eyes stopped at the closet door. It stood wide open.

"Huh?"

65

I lowered my gaze to the foot of my bed—and uttered a cry of shock.

Slappy!

Slappy lay stretched out on his back on top of the bedspread. His eyes, open wide. His red-lipped grin, spread over his wooden face.

17

I burst into Willow's room and shouted, "You're not funny!"

She was already dressed. She sat on the edge of her bed, tying one of her sneakers. Startled by my shout, she let go of the shoelaces. "Funny?"

"You heard me," I said, storming up to her. "You just can't stop with the jokes—*can* you!"

She stood up and pushed me away from her. "I don't know what you're talking about, Richard. I don't know about any jokes." She sighed. "I was up all night. I didn't sleep a wink, and—"

"And so you sneaked into my room and moved Slappy back to my bed," I said. "Very funny. You're a riot, Willow."

She pushed me again with both hands. "Listen to me, okay? Read my lips. I didn't play any joke on you last night."

I studied her face. She seemed to be telling the truth.

"What got you all steamed?" she asked. "What about Slappy? Did you have another nightmare?"

I shook my head. "No. No nightmare. But when I woke up just now, Slappy was on my bed. Down at the bottom where I always put him."

She squinted at me. "But we closed him up in the closet," she replied. "You said you put blankets on top of him."

"You saw me do it," I said. "And then you sneaked into my room—"

"I swear." She raised her right hand. "I didn't play a joke on you. This is no time for jokes, Richard. This is serious."

"Tell me something I don't know," I groaned. "I don't believe—"

I stopped because Mom shouted from the kitchen for us to come to breakfast.

Willow bent down and tied her sneaker laces. "You said Slappy was your friend," she said.

"He's not my friend anymore," I replied. "But I refuse to believe the dummy is alive."

We walked silently to the kitchen. Mom was spooning scrambled eggs from a big pan onto our plates. "What were you two arguing about so heatedly?" she demanded.

"We weren't arguing," I answered. "We were discussing."

"Discussing what?" she asked.

"Slappy," I said.

Mom carried the pan to the sink. "Oh no. Did you have another nightmare? Willow? Did you have a nightmare, too?"

Willow hesitated. "Well . . . we both dreamed that

Slappy took us to the gym to mess up our mural," she said. "In my dream, he forced me to paint his face on the mural."

"He wanted me to paint his face on the mural, too. And he splashed cans of paint on me until I nearly drowned," I said. I shuddered. The dream stayed vivid in my mind.

Mom ran cold water into the pan. Then she joined us at the table. "You've got me stumped," she said. "I'm the sleep expert. I should be able to figure out what's going on. But I don't have a clue."

"These eggs are good, Mom," I said. "Nice and salty, the way I like them."

She frowned at me. "Richard, are you trying to change the subject?"

"Yes," I said. "The whole Slappy thing is too weird. I don't want to talk about it anymore."

"Let's talk about Brandy's birthday party now," Willow said.

I swallowed a chunk of scrambled eggs. "Huh? Birthday party?"

"Don't tell me you forgot," Willow said. "It's tomorrow."

"I *did* forget," I said. "With all these nightmares and no sleep, I can't remember *anything*!"

"Did you get her a present?" Willow asked.

"No," I answered. "What should I get her?"

Willow chuckled. "How about a frog? Since you ate her last one?"

"Not funny," I said. "You know I didn't eat it. You have a sick sense of humor, Willow."

"Thank you," she replied.

"I'm meeting your dad later and doing my Saturday shopping," Mom said. "I'll look for something nice for Brandy." She took a long sip of coffee. "What did you get her, Willow?"

"This awesome illustrated edition of *A Wrinkle in Time*. It's her favorite book."

"Nice," Mom said. "And what are you two doing today? Any Saturday activities planned?"

"We're going to school to finish our mural," I told her. "Miss Deaver wants to take it to the zoo so they have plenty of time to hang it before our overnight."

"Take a photo of it," Mom said. "Your dad and I really want to see it." She stood up and started out of the kitchen. "Finish your breakfast and I'll drive you to school."

Willow hurried to her room. I finished my eggs and washed them down with half a glass of orange juice. I started to stand up when my phone rang. I read the ID on the screen: *Brandy*.

"Hey, Richard, what's up?" she said. "You're coming to my party tomorrow, right?"

"For sure," I said. "We were just talking about it."

"Well, I wanted to ask you something," Brandy continued. "Please don't say no."

Uh-oh.

"We decided to have a talent contest at the party," Brandy said. "And I wondered if you would bring that funny-looking dummy you brought to school and do a ventriloquist act."

"Bring Slappy?" I asked.

"Yeah. Slappy. Is that his name? Everyone is going to do some kind of act, and it would be awesome if you did a funny one with that guy."

"But—but—" I sputtered. "I really don't like to perform, Brandy. I get all tongue-tied and—"

"I know you're shy," she said. "But everyone would love it, Richard. Do it for *me*, okay? For my birthday?"

"I . . . I'll have to think about it," I said.

"Oh, thank you!" she gushed. "I *knew* you'd do it."

A heavy feeling of dread suddenly weighed me down. "What is my cousin going to do?" I asked Brandy.

"Willow? She said she's rapping."

"Huh? I didn't know Willow did rap music."

"I've got to run," Brandy said. "See you tomorrow. Don't forget to bring Sloppy."

"It's *Slappy*," I said. But she had already hung up.

Mom and Willow were already in the car. I grabbed my coat and hurried to join them.

"Did you know about Brandy's talent show?" I asked Willow as Mom backed down the drive.

"Oh, yeah," Willow said. "I forgot to tell you."

"Did you know she wants me to do some kind of act with Slappy?" I demanded.

"No. We didn't talk about you," Willow replied. "Only about me. Are you going to bring him?"

"Do I have a choice?" I said.

"Maybe if you do a comedy act with the dummy, your nightmares will stop," Mom said.

"Maybe . . . ," I muttered.

A few minutes later, she dropped us off at school.

71

The front hall was empty because it was the week-end. We passed by a few classrooms where kids were taking Saturday classes.

The lights were on in the gym. I pushed open the double doors and waited for my eyes to adjust to the bright lights. Pulling off our coats, Willow and I scrambled to the far wall to work on our mural.

But we stopped halfway there—

—and stared in horror.

"Nooooo!" I wailed. "This . . . this can't be true!"

Willow slapped both hands over her head. "I . . . don't believe it!" she cried.

18

I gaped, wide-eyed, at the huge puddle of blue paint splattered over the gym floor. The paint glistened brightly and splashed up like a blue wave onto the wall. Against the wall, blue paint cans lay on their sides.

I raised my eyes to the mural. It was a blur of blue paint at first. And then it slowly came into focus. An enormous head was painted over everything. The head was six feet tall, covering the whole mural.

Slappy's grinning head.

"Our dreams . . . ," Willow murmured, her hands still on the sides of her face, her eyes wide with disbelief. "Our nightmares . . . come true!"

I shook my head. "Dreams don't come true," I choked out. "Somebody did this. Somebody sneaked into the gym and painted that face and splashed paint all over the floor."

"No," Willow said. "Who would do something so horrible? No one. We dreamed it, and it came true, Richard."

"Maybe we're dreaming right now," I said. I stared at the grinning dummy face on the mural.

"Maybe this is another nightmare, Willow. We're going to wake up from this, and it will have never happened."

She stared at me and didn't reply.

"Let's try real hard to wake up," I said. I shut my eyes. "Wake up, Richard," I said out loud. "You are dreaming. Wake up. Wake up—*now*."

I opened my eyes. Nothing had changed.

Willow sighed. "We're doomed," she muttered. "We'll be blamed. No one will believe we didn't do this. We're going to be suspended for this. Maybe we'll be kicked out of school for good."

I swallowed. My mouth suddenly felt as dry as cotton. The sharp smell of the paint was making me dizzy. "Can we clean it up?" I said. "We can at least try to clean the floor, can't we?"

Willow shrugged. "I guess. But it won't be easy."

"Let's check out the custodians' supply closet in the basement," I said. "We can get mops and buckets and—"

I stopped with a gasp when I heard the gym doors bang open. Willow cried out and her eyes went wide.

We both spun around to see someone enter the gym and come striding toward us.

Miss Deaver!

We were caught.

19

"What are you doing here on a Saturday?" The words burst from my mouth before I even thought about them.

I could feel my face grow red-hot. My heart was pounding so hard, I thought it might leap into my throat. Willow froze like a statue with her hands straight out at her sides.

Miss Deaver had her eyes on the mural. Her footsteps rang out loudly against the high gym wall. She wore jeans under her blue down parka.

"I left the test papers in my room," she said. "I had to come get them. I thought I heard someone in here and—*Oh, good heavens!*"

She stared at the enormous blue stain splotched over the floor and the wall. "H-how did that happen?" she stammered. "How did you *do* that?"

"We...uh..." I couldn't think of an answer. When I'm in a jam, I get totally tongue-tied. I can *never* think of the right thing to say. Never.

"Willow? Richard? Please explain," the teacher demanded. "This is a horrible mess. Why did you *do* this?"

My face grew even hotter. My legs felt weak, about to collapse. "Uh . . ."

My mind spun. I couldn't think of a thing. Not a thing. I couldn't tell her our nightmares caused this. No way. If only I could think of something . . .

"It was an accident," Willow said.

Miss Deaver squinted at her. "An accident?"

Willow nodded. "I'm still shaking," she said. "I got up on the ladder to paint the sky. I carried the paint can up with me. But it started to slip from my hand. I grabbed for it, and the ladder fell over."

She let out a sob. "I was so scared, Miss Deaver. I fell on my side, and the paint splashed everywhere."

"Are you okay?" the teacher asked.

"Yes, I'm okay," Willow said. She clutched her side. "I don't think I broke anything. But I feel terrible about the mess. Richard and I were just talking about how we were going to clean it up. Weren't we, Richard?"

"Uh . . . yes, we were," I said.

"You should never climb that ladder when no one else is in school," Miss Deaver scolded. She shook her head. "What's that huge face painted on your zoo mural?"

"We were just messing around," Willow said. "Trying some new paints. We're going to paint over it, aren't we, Richard?"

"Uh . . . yes," I said.

"Well, don't worry about cleaning up the mess," the teacher said. "I'll ask the custodial staff to do it on Monday." She took Willow's arm. "Let me drive you home. You're sure you didn't break anything?"

"I'm okay. Really," Willow said.

So Miss Deaver drove us to my house. I waited until we were in my room to let out a long sigh of relief. "Wow, that was awesome, Willow!" I cried.

"Sometimes it's helpful to be a really good liar," she said.

We both laughed. "Talk about a close call," I said.

Willow frowned. "We got out of trouble. But we're still in trouble," she said. "We didn't clear up the mystery at all."

We both turned to Slappy. The dummy was sitting up at the foot of the bed, just where I had left him.

I walked over to the bed. "Did you do it, Slappy?" I demanded. "Did you somehow make that mess in the gym?"

A crazy thought. But what else could explain it?

I started to pick the dummy up. But I stopped with a cry.

"Oh no," I murmured. "Willow, come look at this. Slappy's hands. What are those spots? Are those blue paint stains on his hands?"

20

I'm not very good at parties, even when it's all kids I know. And I felt seriously uncomfortable bringing Slappy to Brandy's party.

Yes, I did think Slappy was a friend. But that was *before* all the nightmares began. Now I thought of the dummy as some kind of evil horror-movie creature.

I was actually afraid of him.

Afraid to go to sleep at night. Afraid during the daytime, too. Did we really bring him to life? Did he ruin our mural at school?

I kept thinking about the blue paint stains on his hands. I saw the ruined mural every time I closed my eyes. We had to throw it out. There was no time to paint another one.

I was living a nightmare. And I had no way to explain it—or stop it!

I wanted to leave him at home. I didn't want to bring him to a party. But Willow said Brandy would be very disappointed. Also, she said if I didn't do a ventriloquist act with Slappy, what would my talent be?

I understood what Willow was saying. She meant that I *have* no talent. And I guess she's right. I mean, *not everyone* has to be talented—do they?

Maybe my talent is putting up with Willow and all her tricks.

But I spent most of Saturday afternoon in my room, practicing a comedy act with Slappy. I'm not good with jokes, and I really wanted Willow to help me think of some.

But she was busy rehearsing her song in her room and couldn't help me.

I didn't want to be holding Slappy. What if he came to life on my lap? What evil would he do? I couldn't believe it, but I was actually terrified of a wooden dummy.

So, when Dad dropped us off at Brandy's house for the party on Sunday afternoon, I was even more stressed out than usual.

The party was downstairs in Brandy's huge basement rec room. As I followed Willow down the stairs, I saw that a lot of kids from our class were already there.

I dropped Slappy behind a big pile of wrapped birthday presents and gazed around. Willow was already talking and laughing with two of her friends.

A food table stretched along one wall with a stack of pizza boxes at one end. A tall, pink-and-white birthday cake stood beside the pizza boxes.

Old childhood photos of Brandy flashed by on the flatscreen TV on the wall. The shouts and laughter of the kids nearly drowned out the music from two speakers in the ceiling.

Brandy wore a sparkly vest over a green sweater and bright green leggings. Brandy's eyes are green, so guess what her favorite color is?

She carried two presents wrapped in tissue paper and dumped them with the other gifts. Then she turned to me. "Hey, Richard, how's it going?"

"Okay," I said. "Happy birthday."

"Did you bring Sloppy?" she asked.

"It's *Slappy*," I said. "Yes. I brought him."

"The talent show is going to be awesome!" Brandy gushed. "We have such a talented class. Do you want to go first?"

I nearly choked. "Huh? Me? First? I don't know. I—"

She laughed. "You don't have to." She pointed to Lisi Franklin across the room. "Lisi brought her violin. Did you know she plays in the youth orchestra? She's like what they call a prodigy."

"A prodigy?" I repeated.

Brandy nodded. "Yeah. She's *amazing*!"

"Please don't make me go on after *her*!" I said.

I don't think Brandy heard me. She took off toward the stairs to greet two boys who were waving to her.

When the party guests were all there, Brandy's parents passed out paper plates with pizza to everyone. Lisi Franklin said she had a food allergy and couldn't have cheese. So Brandy's dad carefully tried to pull the cheese off her pizza, but she couldn't eat it anyway.

I wasn't very hungry. My stomach felt like it was tied in a knot. I couldn't stop thinking about the act

I was supposed to do with Slappy. I knew my jokes were terrible and everyone would totally make fun of me. Why did I ever agree to it?

And now that I thought Slappy was alive, it was a thousand times worse. I kept checking to make sure he hadn't moved from where I'd dropped him behind the pile of birthday presents.

"We'll open presents after the talent show," Brandy said. "Then we'll have the birthday cake. Let's get started."

We all sat down on the floor, facing the food table. Brandy made us back up so there was space for kids to perform. I picked up Slappy and held him in my lap near the wall.

It took a while for everyone to quiet down. Brandy raised a small package wrapped in silver paper. "This is the prize for the winning act," she said.

"What is it?" Cory Feld asked from the front row.

"A surprise," Brandy said. "Hey, Cory, you can go first."

A few kids cheered as Cory stood up and moved to the performing space. He took out a tiny metal harmonica, stuck it between his lips, and played a pretty good blues song.

Everyone clapped and hooted when he finished it. "How did I do?" Cory asked Brandy.

"At least you didn't swallow it!" she answered. Brandy can be pretty cold when she wants to be.

Lea Smith and Kamesha Gardener sang an old Beatles song together. They were very good. Angelo Camini did some card tricks. He was nervous and the cards kept fluttering onto the floor. Lisi Franklin played a long violin solo, and everyone went nuts, cheering and screaming. It was so awesome!

"Okay, Richard," Brandy said finally. "It's your turn. Richard is going to do a ventriloquist act with his friend Sloppy," she announced.

I climbed to my feet. My throat suddenly felt dry, and my legs were shaky. I stepped between a bunch of kids and carried Slappy to the front of the crowd.

Here goes, I told myself.

21

I sat down on a low wooden stool and put Slappy on my lap. "This is my friend Slappy," I said. My voice shook a bit. I couldn't hide how nervous I was. "Some of you probably remember the time I brought this dummy to school."

"*Who's the dummy?*" I made Slappy say in a shrill, tinny voice.

A few kids laughed. It made me feel a little braver.

"Slappy, what is your favorite subject in school?" I asked him.

I pulled the string inside his back and made his mouth move up and down. "*Woodworking Shop,*" I made him say.

"Is that because your head is made of wood?" I asked him.

"*No. It's because I want to build myself a girlfriend!*"

A few kids laughed at that, but not many.

I thought it was a pretty good joke. But I could see my act was not exactly a hit. My heart started to pound, and I felt cold sweat drip down my forehead.

"Slappy, can you say happy birthday to Brandy?" I asked him.

"*Only if you move my lips!*" I made him say.

Willow laughed at that one. But nobody else did.

My mind suddenly went blank. I felt a jolt of panic. I couldn't remember what came next. What was my next joke?

While I struggled to remember, something strange happened. Something strange and frightening.

The dummy spoke up *on his own.*

"*Richard, do you know how to make me yawn? Your jokes are putting me to sleep!*"

"Huh?" A startled gasp escaped my throat.

A few kids laughed.

"Hey—I didn't make him say that!" I told the audience.

"*Maybe I should take a turn working YOUR head!*" the dummy exclaimed.

"This isn't happening!" I cried. "He's . . . he's talking on his own!"

A bunch of kids laughed. They thought I was joking.

Willow squinted at me, as if to say, *What's going on?*

Sitting right in front of me, Brandy shook her head. I could see she was not thrilled with my act.

"*You're putting EVERYONE to sleep!*" Slappy shouted. "*Let's all take a nap!*"

Both of his hands shot straight up. "*Nap time, kids! You're feeling sleepy. Your eyelids are getting heavy. You can't keep your eyes open any longer. You are falling asleep . . . asleep . . . asleep.*"

84

I suddenly felt drowsy. I wanted to toss Slappy off my lap and put an end to whatever was going on. But instead, I opened my mouth in a long yawn. My arms felt heavy. My head drooped.

"*. . . Asleep . . . You are all going to sleep. Good night, everyone. Enjoy your nap . . .*"

I struggled to stay awake. But I was fading . . .

"*Nap time, everyone. See you in your dreams!*"

Kids yawned. I saw Brandy stretch out on the floor and close her eyes. Everyone was sinking to the floor, sprawling on their sides, their backs. Willow tucked herself into a ball and fell asleep.

That was the last thing I saw before I fell asleep, too. A heavy silence hung over the huge rec room. No one moved. Slumped on the stool, my arms dangled to the floor as I sank into a deep sleep.

How long was I out?

I have no idea. It could have been minutes. It could have been hours.

But the next thing I knew, someone had my shoulder and was waking me up. I opened my eyes. Slappy stood in front of me, shaking me with his wooden hand.

"*Wake up, Richard. We have work to do.*"

22

"You—you're alive!" I cried. "You're really alive!"

"*Get over it*," the dummy snapped. "*Stand up. We have work to do.*"

"Work?" I was still blinking, still trying to pull myself out of the blackness of sleep.

"*Before they wake up*," Slappy said, motioning to the floor of sleeping kids with one hand. "*Get moving.*"

I climbed to my feet. "You are standing up on your own," I said. "How are you doing that?"

"*The same way you are!*" he replied. "*Hurry, servant. Look at all the birthday presents in that pile.*"

"Brandy's presents," I said. "What about them?"

"*You have to open them*," he said, giving me a push on the back. "*Hurry. You have to open them all!*"

"But—but—" I sputtered. "I can't do that. Those are Brandy's."

"*You have no choice!*" the dummy screamed. "*You are my servant! Open them! Let's see if there's anything we want to keep!*"

86

He waved a hand in front of my face, and I felt a strong force pulling me toward the stack of birthday presents. I tried to push back. But the force was too powerful.

I stumbled up to the presents and picked up a box with yellow-and-white gift wrapping.

"Hurry! Open it!" Slappy screamed, waving his arms in the air.

"Please—no," I said. But my hands were already tearing at the wrapping paper. I ripped the paper away and pulled open the box.

I gazed at the silky brown sweater inside.

"Garbage!" Slappy declared. *"Throw it away. What's next?"*

The next package contained two graphic novels.

"Next!" the dummy cried.

I tore off the wrapping on a set of twenty-four colored markers. "Why are we doing this?" I demanded. "This isn't right!"

"Next!" Slappy cried.

I opened a few more presents. The torn wrapping paper cluttered the floor all around me. Presents were scattered everywhere.

When I opened the last gift in the pile—two pairs of bright green tights—Slappy tossed back his head and laughed. *"Richard, you made a mess!"* he exclaimed. *"Why did you do this? Why did you open your friend's presents?"*

"You! You made me do it!" I cried.

He cackled again, the raspy sound echoing off the low basement ceiling.

"*Let's try the cake before everyone wakes up,*" Slappy said.

"No way," I said. "I won't do it, Slappy. Seriously. I won't—"

But again, I felt the force pulling me across the floor. I pulled back, but I didn't have the strength to fight it.

I stepped up to the food table and gazed at the tall cake.

"*Go ahead. Take a big handful,*" Slappy ordered.

"No. Please—"

"*Take a handful, Richard!*"

I reached my hand out toward the cake.

But I pulled it back quickly when I heard a thunder of footsteps. I turned to see Brandy's mom coming down the basement stairs.

Mrs. Linker stopped two-thirds of the way down. I caught the confusion on her face when she saw that the kids were all sound asleep on the rec room floor.

And then her mouth dropped open when she saw the gift wrapping ripped up and scattered everywhere. The presents tossed over the floor.

It took her a few seconds to see me standing at the table in front of the birthday cake. "Richard? What is *happening* here?" she cried. "I don't understand!"

"*Pick up the cake!*" Slappy ordered, screaming into my ear. "*Pick it up. Hurry. Let her have it!*"

I didn't have the strength to fight his strange power. My hands seemed to move on their own.

I slid my hands under the cake and lifted it off the table.

"*Let her have it!*" the dummy ordered.

I carried the cake to the stairs. Then I stepped up beside Mrs. Linker. I raised the cake high—and *smashed* it over her head.

She shrieked as the gooey cake oozed down over her head, her shoulders . . .

She frantically tore clumps of cake from her face. "Richard!" she choked out. "Richard! Richard!"

23

"Richard! Richard! Richard!"

I felt a hand shaking me by the shoulder.

I blinked open my eyes and saw Brandy's mom leaning over me, eyes wide with alarm. "Richard— wake up! You fell asleep sitting on the stool." She gazed around. "Why did everyone go to sleep?"

The room tilted and spun in front of me. I struggled to my feet.

What is happening? Was I dreaming again?

All over the floor, Brandy's party guests were waking up, groaning and yawning. Kids sat up slowly, shaking their heads in confusion.

I turned toward the pile of birthday gifts. They were all neatly wrapped, stacked as they had been before I faded out.

I let out a long breath. "Wheww."

A nightmare. Ripping apart the presents had been a nightmare.

But I hadn't dreamed about the kids falling asleep. That was real. I stood and watched them all sitting up, blinking and rubbing their eyes, shaking their heads, totally confused.

Slappy did this, I told myself. *Slappy put everyone in this room to sleep.*

Where was he?

He had been in my lap. I had been performing my lame comedy act with him. And then he had taken over and—

"Oh noooo!"

I spotted the dummy on the floor next to the stool. He was sitting straight up, his legs spread. And the cake . . . The birthday cake was smashed to bits—in his lap.

Big chunks of cake all around where he sat. And an oozing heap of cake and icing piled in his lap.

"How did this HAPPEN?" Mrs. Linker's voice rang off the low ceiling. "Can anyone explain to me? What HAPPENED here?"

"I had a terrible nightmare," Brandy said, striding up to her mom.

"So did I!" Lisi Franklin cried.

"So did I!" a bunch of other kids chimed in.

"I had this horrible dream about Richard's dummy!" Brandy told her mom.

"So did I! So did I!" The voices rang off the walls.

Mrs. Linker hugged Brandy and then turned to me. "Richard, can you explain this?"

I shook my head. Panic choked my throat. "N-no," I stammered. "I can't."

"My birthday cake—!" Brandy cried. "It's *ruined*! Wrecked! Richard, how *could* you?"

"I . . . I didn't," I said, my voice cracking on the words.

Everyone began shouting at once. Kids were telling one another the nightmares they'd had about Slappy.

Willow came up to me and pulled me toward the stairs. "We both know the dummy did this," she said. "We both know he put everyone to sleep and then gave them Slappy nightmares."

"I . . . I know," I said.

Willow brought her face close to my ear and whispered, "The question is, what are we going to do about it?"

SLAPPY HERE, EVERYONE.

Hahaha. That's the question everyone always asks.

What are we going to do about Slappy?

The answer is simple. Admire him! Praise him! Applaud him! Congratulate him for being so brilliant! And mainly, *obey* him! Hahaha.

What else can Richard and Willow do?

The electrodes in his mother's sleep lab gave me an electric jolt. I was asleep, but suddenly, I had the power to invade dreams. Thank you very much for hooking me up, Richard's mother! Hahaha.

And then Richard and Willow read the secret words and woke me up.

So now I can destroy them when they're awake—*and* when they're asleep! Hahaha!

You might as well stop reading here, everyone. You already know who the winner is in *this* story!

24

Dad picked Willow and me up from Brandy's house. I can always tell when he's angry or upset because his cheeks get bright pink. And believe me, they were bright pink now.

"Let's not talk till we get home," he said. "Your mom is waiting. We need to have a family discussion."

We only have family discussions when I'm in major trouble. And, of course, I was in major trouble with a capital T-R-O-U-B-L-E. I knew that Mrs. Linker had called my parents and told them about Brandy's birthday cake.

Mom was waiting for us at the front door. When she's angry and upset, Mom is the opposite of Dad. She doesn't turn pink. She goes pale as milk and bites her bottom lip till it bleeds.

"You have a lot of explaining to do, Richard," she said as I followed Willow into the house.

How can I explain anything? I wondered. *I can't explain it to myself!*

I dumped Slappy on the floor in the entryway. My parents marched Willow and me to the den. We sat side by side on the couch, and they both perched on the big armchair facing us.

"Mrs. Linker called," Mom started. She clasped her hands tensely in her lap, another bad sign. "She said that you hypnotized all the kids and made them go to sleep."

"Huh?" I jumped to my feet. "Me? Hypnotize?"

"Sit down, Richard," Dad said. "Don't act surprised."

"But—but—" I sputtered.

Mom bit her bottom lip. "Mrs. Linker said that when the kids woke up, Brandy's birthday cake was smashed to bits. She said you made it look as if the dummy had done it."

"Mom, I couldn't help it." I jumped to my feet again. "The dummy *did* do it!" I cried.

Dad motioned me down with both hands. "Sit, Richard. Let's talk about this seriously. And stop the nonsense."

"Slappy is alive!" I cried. "I'm not talking nonsense. He's alive, and he can get into everyone's dreams. And *he* is the one who smashed Brandy's cake."

Mom rolled her eyes. "Oh, please," she groaned. "Give me a break."

Dad turned to Willow. "What did you see? Did you see the dummy come alive and wreck the birthday cake?"

Willow glanced at me, then shook her head. "I didn't see anything. I was asleep."

Dad's cheeks turned a darker pink. "You were asleep? It's really true? Everyone fell asleep?"

Willow nodded. "Yeah. I guess we did."

"But I didn't hypnotize them!" I exclaimed. "I don't know how to hypnotize people. I was doing my stupid comedy act with Slappy in front of everyone, and—"

"I know the first thing we have to do," Dad interrupted. "We have to put that dummy away somewhere for a while. We have to lock him up. And you have to forget about him. I know you think he's your friend, Richard, but—"

"He's not a friend anymore," I said. "He's too scary. I haven't slept in days, and my nightmares—"

"Me too," Willow said. "I have nightmares about Slappy, too."

"I know you don't believe me," I said. "But the dummy was the one who put everyone to sleep and—"

"No more talk," Dad said, jumping to his feet. "Let's solve this problem right away. Follow me."

Willow and I followed him to the front entryway. He grabbed Slappy by one leg and carried him upside down to the basement stairs. Dad clicked on the lights, and we followed him to the basement.

We don't have a big rec room downstairs like Brandy. Our basement looks like a basement. It's gray and dusty and smells bad, with cartons stacked everywhere and old furniture piled high, and a mess of junk. The furnace rattled and the hot water heater churned noisily.

Still holding him by one leg, Dad carried the dummy past a clutter of old clothes and a stack of yellowing newspapers. He stopped at a large black trunk against the wall. It was the kind of trunk that looked like a pirate treasure chest with a metal clasp on the lid.

Dad handed Slappy to me. Then he turned and struggled to open the clasp. It was rusted shut, and he had to work at it for a while. Finally, he lifted the big lid.

A sour smell rose to greet us. "Who is buried in here?" Willow joked.

Dad didn't laugh.

I peered at the folded-up clothes in the trunk. An old army uniform jacket and some sweaters that seemed to be half-decayed.

Dad pushed the stack of sweaters aside and took Slappy from me. He lowered Slappy into the trunk, folded him up, and covered him with moldy old sweaters. Then he carefully forced the latch shut.

Dad smacked his hands together, wiping off dust. "That takes care of the dummy problem," he said. "Of course, you are also grounded, Richard."

Grounded? I didn't care. All I could think was, *Finally I'm going to get a good night's sleep.*

Mom was waiting upstairs. "We still have to get you and Willow packed for the zoo overnight," she said. "You can be gounded when you get back. Willow, we have an extra sleeping bag. So you won't have to go home for one."

Willow grinned at me. "I guess you won't be taking Slappy to the zoo."

"You're not funny," I muttered. "Slappy will not be invited anywhere for a loooong time."

97

That night, Willow wanted to stay up and watch music videos on YouTube. But I said *no way*. I got changed for bed early. And I turned out the bedroom light and tucked myself in with a smile.

I closed my eyes and faded into sleep almost instantly.

And there was Slappy, waiting for me.

He brought his face up against mine. His eyes blazed red, like fire. His eyebrows appeared to rise up high on his forehead. And he hissed at me: *"You'll be sssssssorry!"*

"Please—" I begged.

"You'll be sssssorry, Richard. I'm going to haunt your dreams . . . FOREVER!"

"Ohhh!" I woke up with a choked cry.

I sat up, blinking, chills running down my back. I peered into the darkness. And uttered another cry.

Slappy sat grinning at me from the foot of the bed.

25

The next morning, Willow and I were yawning as we tossed our sleeping bags and backpacks into the storage bins on the side of the school bus.

It was a clear, cold morning. The sun was still a red ball floating low in the sky. Brown leaves crunched under our sneakers as we made our way onto the bus.

Kids shouted out greetings to us as Willow and I squeezed down the aisle. The bus was already nearly full.

I said good morning to Brandy, and she spun her head away from me. I could see she was still angry about her birthday party.

Willow and I found a seat near the back of the bus. "I hope you enjoyed ruining my birthday cake!" Brandy shouted.

"I—I didn't," I stammered. "I—"

"And I hope you left that disgusting dummy at home!" Brandy yelled.

"Of course I did," I called. She turned her head away again. I guessed she planned to stay mad at me for life.

Willow and I settled back in our seat. I yawned. "I was up all night," I told her.

"Me too," she groaned. "It took hours to fall asleep, and then I had another nightmare about Slappy. I woke up shaking."

The bus hit a bump and everybody jumped.

"Maybe we'll finally get some sleep tonight at the zoo," I said.

Willow snickered. "Unless the monkeys stay up chattering all night."

Miss Deaver stood up at her seat in the front. "Our zoo guide is a woman named Estrella," she announced. "She is going to give us a complete tour of the zoo first thing."

"Do we get to feed any animals?" a boy named Harry Winters asked.

"Maybe after lunch," Miss Deaver said.

"Who is going to feed Harry?" a girl in the front row asked.

A lot of kids laughed. It was funny because Harry is always talking about food.

"The zoo is very large and spread out," Miss Deaver said. "I don't want anyone wandering off on your own. I want you all to pick a partner, so we'll always go around in twos."

Kids started shouting across the aisle, getting partners.

I turned to Willow. "Want to be my partner?"

"I already promised Brandy," she said.

I knew what that meant. That meant my partner would be Andy Popper. Andy was the other shy kid in class. He never said a word. And when he did speak, his voice was so soft, the words just dribbled down his chin and no one could hear him.

Andy and I ended up as partners a lot.

He was probably a good guy. But there was no way to tell since I almost never heard what he said.

Estrella and other zoo workers were waiting for us when the bus pulled into the zoo parking lot. She was a young woman with short black hair, big dark eyes, and a nice smile. The zoo workers all wore blue caps and bright blue vests over white sweaters.

Estrella had a clipboard in her hand and checked off our names as we climbed off the bus. "Stay with your partners," she said. "We have a lot of ground to cover."

"What about lunch?" Harry Winters asked. "Is that before or after the tour?"

"After," Estrella said. "And don't worry about your bags. My friends here are unloading the bus. They'll take everything to the Ape and Monkey House, where you'll be sleeping."

Estrella led the way into the zoo grounds. Miss Deaver walked beside her. The rest of us followed in twos. Andy and I tried to stay close to Estrella so we could hear what she was telling us about the animals.

Our town is small, but the zoo is the largest in the state. People come here from cities and towns all around.

We all loved the Penguin House. The penguins were behind tall glass windows. They live on a giant iceberg surrounded by water. They have a great life, waddling on the ice, then diving into the water for a swim.

Across the way from the penguins, the seals also had an awesome habitat. They live on a tall rock island with caves for them to hide in. It is also surrounded by water.

While we were watching, two zoo workers came with big buckets of fish and tossed the fish one by one to the seals. Andy said something about how good the seals were at catching the fish. But I couldn't really hear him over the splash and loud honking of the seals and the voices of the other kids.

I guess if I had to choose, the Jungle Habitat was my favorite part of the zoo. It was designed to be like a jungle in India. And the animals roamed free in the habitat. We watched from behind a wall as two trainers led out the zoo's Bengal tigers.

The tigers strained at the rope leashes the trainers held them by. They growled and bared their long teeth. They were big enough to be really scary!

"The Bengal tigers are just about the biggest wildcats still alive," Estrella explained. "We are lucky here. These are young males. They weigh a little over four hundred pounds, and they are still growing."

"What do they eat?" Harry Winters asked.

"Whatever they want!" Estrella laughed at her own joke.

"We are very lucky to have these two because, sadly, tigers are an endangered species."

One of the tigers let out an angry growl, showing

us how tough he was. The other one dug restlessly at the sand with his front paws.

The zoo also has giraffes. Estrella told us giraffes sleep less than two hours a day. She asked for a volunteer to feed one. Of course, my cousin Willow was the first to raise her hand and shout, "Me! Me!"

Estrella handed Willow a bucket of carrots, and Willow tossed the carrots into the giraffe's open mouth. The animal chewed them up noisily and swallowed them.

It was an awesome day. I think everyone had fun. That evening, we ate a pizza dinner in the Ape and Monkey House. The monkeys hopped around their tree branches and chattered as if they were excited, too.

It was a cold night, and there wasn't much heat there. Miss Deaver said, "You'll be nice and warm in your sleeping bags."

The bags had been piled against one wall. We all scrambled to get our stuff. The boys spread out their sleeping bags by the chimpanzee and monkey cages near the front. The girls spread theirs out by the orangutan cages at the back of the room.

I tossed my backpack to the floor and claimed a spot by the wall. Two chimpanzees watched me with their noses pressed to their cage bars.

"Don't stare," I muttered. But they didn't move.

I untied my sleeping bag and started to unroll it over the floor.

I had it half-open when I stopped with a startled gasp.

"Oh no!" I cried. "What are *you* doing here?"

26

I stared at Slappy, snuggled on his back in the sleep-ing bag. His eyes were shut and his grin was wide, as if he was having a pleasant dream.

Or enjoying his little joke on me.

I grabbed him by the shoulders and tugged him from the bag. "How did you get here? Did someone stuff you in there?"

The dummy's eyes opened wide. I shook him hard. "I don't want you here. How did you get here?"

The two monkeys were still staring at me. Some kids were watching me, too.

I picked up Slappy, slung him over my shoulder, and carried him to the other end of the room, where some girls were unrolling their sleeping bags. "Willow? Hey, Willow?" I shouted across the room to her.

She spun around—and saw Slappy. "Oh nooo," she moaned.

"Did you put him in my bag?" I demanded. "Is this one of your jokes?"

She raised her right hand. "No. I swear!"

I held Slappy in front of me. "Are you sure?"

"I didn't do it, Richard!" Willow cried. "I don't want him here, either!"

"Take that thing away from here!" Brandy shouted. "Haven't you done enough damage with that ugly doll?"

I stared at Willow a little while longer. I could see she was telling the truth. With a sigh, I turned and trudged back to my sleeping bag against the front wall.

"Don't grin at me like that," I told the dummy. "I'm not going to let you ruin the overnight."

At least the two monkeys had stopped watching. They had disappeared somewhere behind the tree in their cage.

I unzipped my backpack and pulled out the pajamas I had packed. I stuffed Slappy headfirst into the backpack. He didn't quite fit. I folded up his arms and legs and squeezed him toward the bottom. Then I stuffed the pajamas back in on top of him.

I zipped the backpack up tightly. My hands were shaking. My mind was whirring. *What should I do with the backpack?*

I had this crazy idea to stuff it inside one of the monkey cages. That way, the dummy would be trapped behind bars.

But, of course, I couldn't do that. For one thing, the cage bars were too close together.

I crossed to the other side of the big room. And spotted a thick, coiled-up rope on the floor. I picked up the rope. It was heavy and strong. I uncoiled it. Then I wrapped it around the backpack several times and tied the ends into tight knots.

That should hold him, I thought.

I carried the backpack to the other side and shoved it against the wall. Then I tugged off my sneakers and slid into the sleeping bag. Shivering, I pulled myself as deep as I could into it and waited to warm up.

I tried to force Slappy from my mind. It had been a long day, and we had walked miles inside the zoo. I felt my eyelids grow heavy, and before I knew it, I fell into a deep sleep.

How long did I sleep?

I can't say. But Slappy woke me, staring wide-eyed, his face floating above me.

Or was I dreaming? Had he come to me once again in a dream?

"Wake up!" he screeched. His eyebrows flew up and down on his wooden forehead. His eyes appeared to glow. "Wake up, Richard!"

I groaned. I could feel the warmth of the sleeping bag. My weariness weighed me down.

Am I awake? Is this happening for real?

"Wake up!" the dummy demanded. "Hurry. You don't want to miss all the fun—*do* you?"

27

The dummy's shrill, raspy voice rang in my ears. I sat up, blinking myself alert.

"Hurry! Hurry, Richard!" Slappy's eyes rolled crazily in his head.

I started to climb out of the sleeping bag—but then stopped. I stuck out my arm and pinched it as hard as I could.

"Ouch!"

I was awake. Not dreaming.

I scrambled to my feet and grabbed for my sneakers.

The lights in the Ape and Monkey House had been dimmed. I squinted into the gray and saw the other kids stirring. Getting up. Everyone.

I heard groans and whispers all around. I peered to the other side of the long hall and saw Willow and Brandy's group all standing up, too.

I shivered. The air was cool. I could see my breath in front of me as I pulled on my shoes. The monkeys were silent. Were they all asleep? Why were all the kids waking up?

I heard the doors to the habitat bang open. Kids were heading out the door. I pulled on my jacket and followed.

I saw Harry and Andy walking side by side. Their eyes were wide. They didn't blink. Their arms were stretched out in front of them. They walked stiff-legged. Like zombies in a horror movie.

Are they sleepwalking? I asked myself.

No one spoke. The girls were closest to the doors. I saw Willow, eyes wide, arms stiff in front of her, marching... marching alongside Brandy and two other girls... marching out into the night.

"Slappy!" I cried out his name. I didn't see him, but I knew that evil dummy was nearby. "Slappy—what have you done?" My voice rang off the habitat walls.

"Did you invade *everyone's* dreams?" I demanded. "Slappy, are you making everyone walk out of here?"

His cold cackle clattered in my ears. I spun around. I couldn't see him. But I could hear his laugh clearly, close enough to send shivers down my back.

And I could hear his words: "Hurry. Catch up, Richard. You don't want to be left behind. Your class is going to have an awesome *jungle adventure!*"

28

The lights around the zoo were all dimmed to a low glow. The sky was solid black, no moon or stars. The trees shook in a cold, soft breeze.

I looked for Miss Deaver as I followed the kids through the wide lane. I didn't see her. And I didn't see any zoo workers, either.

What is Slappy doing? I asked myself. *He's making the kids all walk together. Where is he taking us?*

The kids all moved like a silent herd of cattle, walking slowly. But all eyes were straight ahead. And no one talked. The scrape of shoes on the pavement was the only sound breaking the strange, frightening silence.

And then that sound vanished as we stepped onto tall grass. The grass led to soft sand. And I knew where Slappy was taking everyone.

He was taking us all to the Jungle Habitat. He was taking us to the home of the tigers!

Yes, there we were in the jungle. The twisted trees looked eerie against the night sky.

Everyone woke up at the same time. Everyone came out of Slappy's trance. Everyone was confused at first, and then their eyes went wide with fright.

Kids lowered their arms. Voices rang out. Kids muttered their surprise to one another.

I jumped as I heard Willow's yell: "The tigers!"

Startled gasps and low cries rang over the marshy sand. I jumped back a few steps as the two Bengal tigers slid out from behind the trees.

Kids froze. I saw Harry Winters fall to his knees. Willow covered her face with her hands. Beside her, Brandy clung tightly to Willow's arm.

The tigers snarled angrily. They lowered their heads and slunk toward us, keeping their bodies low.

I heard Slappy's laugh in my ears. A cold, triumphant laugh.

And then the evil dummy rasped in my ears: "You're all having a real adventure, Richard. You can thank me later—if you survive! Hahahaha!"

The tigers both roared. They reared back on their hind legs.

Preparing to attack.

I opened my mouth in a terrified scream. But no sound came out.

I raised both arms in front of me, as if trying to shield myself.

I couldn't think. I couldn't move. I couldn't breathe.

Screams and terrified shrieks rang in my ears as the snarling tigers both leaped into the air at once.

I shut my eyes. I didn't want to watch.

29

POP POP!

Two soft explosions made me open my eyes.

I watched in shock as the tigers stopped in midair. Their growls cut short, they came down hard, thudding to the sand on their sides. They didn't move.

Kids screamed and staggered back.

One of the tigers groaned and struggled to raise his head. But his eyes closed and he sank back into the sand.

Two white-uniformed zoo workers pushed their way through the crowd of kids. They carried short rifles in front of them as they ran.

"What are you doing out here?" one of them yelled. "It isn't safe here! The tigers!"

"Don't be upset, kids!" the other one shouted. "Tranquilizer darts. We used tranquilizer darts. We just knocked them out."

"Stand back! Stand back!" his partner warned us.

The two men bent to examine the tigers. One of them pulled the darts from the tigers' shoulders. "They'll be okay. Go back, everyone. Go back to the Ape and Monkey House. And stay there."

I turned and saw Miss Deaver running across the pavement toward the Jungle Habitat. "What is happening? What are you *doing* out here?" she screamed with her hands cupped around her mouth as she ran.

Frozen in shock, the kids all gazed at one another. None of them knew how to answer her questions.

I knew the answer. And maybe Willow did, too.

I knew that Slappy had used his dream powers to put everyone in a trance, to make them walk into the tigers' den.

Miss Deaver didn't wait for anyone to answer her. She just kept asking questions. "Did someone bring you here? Why did you all wake up? What got into your heads? How could you do something so dangerous?"

Frantically, she began to wave us toward the Ape and Monkey House. "Let's go, everyone. Hurry! Get back to your sleeping bags."

I glanced around. Kids still looked dazed and confused. No one spoke. We all started to walk out of the Jungle Habitat.

I heard a long, low moan behind me. I turned and saw that the tigers were waking up. The zoo workers hovered over them, making sure they were okay.

I shivered in the cold night air. Willow hurried up beside me. She leaned close and spoke just above a whisper. "It was Slappy, wasn't it?"

I nodded. "Of course it was," I replied. "It had to be."

"He worked his way into everyone's dreams, and he sent us all into the tigers' home."

I nodded. "Yes. That's what he did."

Willow grabbed my arm. "Richard—what are you going to do? You've got to find a way to stop him."

I nodded again and locked my eyes on hers. "Willow," I said, "believe it or not, I have an idea."

30

The next morning, our class had breakfast at the zoo cafeteria. We were all pretty quiet. I think everyone was still shaken and confused.

Miss Deaver stood at the front of the room and asked again if anyone could explain what exactly had happened last night. "Whose idea was it to go out to the Jungle Habitat?" she asked.

Her question was greeted by a heavy silence.

Harry Winters dropped his fork, and it clattered loudly on the concrete floor. A few kids laughed. Otherwise, there was no other sound.

I glanced at Willow down the row of tables. She and I were the only ones who could explain how everyone ended up in such horrible danger at the Jungle Habitat.

But there was *no way* we'd try to tell Miss Deaver the reason. If I said that the dummy invaded our dreams and hypnotized everyone into marching into the tigers' home, would she believe me?

Three guesses.

Miss Deaver would accuse me of making a joke of

the whole thing. And the other kids would all have a good laugh at poor, twisted Richard.

So Willow and I kept our mouths shut. And Miss Deaver kept shaking her head and muttering to Estrella. And the whole thing remained a frightening mystery.

After breakfast, we packed up and piled into the school bus to leave. The bus dropped Willow off at her house. Her parents had returned the night before.

When the bus stopped at my house, I went racing up the front lawn and burst into the house. I tossed the sleeping bag and backpack on the floor and shouted for my parents.

"Anyone home? Hey—anyone home?"

Mom walked out of the kitchen, wiping her hands on a dish towel. "Richard, you're home early," she said. "Your dad's at work. I thought—"

"I need to ask you a big favor," I said.

"But how was the sleepover?" she demanded. "Was it fun?"

"It was . . . exciting," I said. I tugged her sleeve. "Listen to me. I need to ask a favor."

"Okay," she said. "A favor. Fine. Why are you so upset? Did something bad happen at the zoo?"

"I need to ask a favor and not explain it to you," I said. I was breathing hard. "Okay? Can I ask this and you promise you won't ask me any questions about it?"

She shook her head. "No. I can't promise that." She squinted hard at me. "Go ahead. Ask your favor, and we'll see."

I took a deep breath. "I want to go back to your sleep lab," I said.

She blinked. "Okay. So far, that's not a big favor."

"I want to bring Slappy again," I said. "And I want you to hook him up to your computers again."

Mom kept her eyes locked on me, waiting for me to finish.

"And . . . and I want you to hook me up, too," I said. "Hook Slappy and me up to the same computers."

"That isn't hard to do," Mom said. "But—why?"

"That's the part I can't explain," I said.

How *could* I tell her my idea?

When Mom hooked Slappy up the first time, she was surprised that he was sending off brain waves. After being hooked up to the sleep lab equipment, Slappy had new powers. He could invade people's dreams. He could appear in their sleep and terrify them—and make them do dangerous things.

My idea was simple.

Mom would hook me up, too. Hook Slappy and me up to the same machine. I would go to sleep. And I would invade Slappy's dreams.

The only way to defeat Slappy for good was to face him and defeat him in his dreams.

Maybe I was totally wrong. Maybe my idea was ridiculous. But I couldn't think of anything else. And . . . it was at least worth a try.

"Mom—please?" I begged.

She frowned at me. "Richard, I'm worried about you and that dummy. You need to make real friends and forget about Slappy."

"I will, Mom. I promise," I said, raising my right hand to swear. "If you do this one favor, I'll get rid of Slappy. Really. I'll never mention him again."

She stared at me for a long while. I could see she was thinking hard.

"Okay," she said finally. "I don't know why I am agreeing to this. But, okay. We'll go tonight."

"Yaaaay. Thank you!" I rushed forward and hugged her.

This was my last chance to get Slappy out of my dreams—and out of my life.

31

"Back again?" Mom's assistant, Salazar, said as I followed Mom into the sleep lab. Salazar grinned at me. "And I see you brought your friend with you."

"He's not my friend," I muttered.

Salazar looked surprised by my answer.

"I have four patients to connect," he said. "Then I'll connect you and your puppet."

And that's how it happened.

That's how Slappy and I came to be covered in electrodes and wired into a computer together. That's how we came to be lying side by side on our backs.

How did I get Slappy back to the sleep lab? I told him that getting hooked up again would give him even stronger powers.

Now here we were. I shut my eyes tight and tried to force all thoughts from my mind. Clear my head and sink into the darkness . . . the deep darkness of sleep.

Darkness . . . A deep well of solid black . . .

And then a flash of bright white light made me gasp.

And Slappy stood before me, bobbing slightly on his flimsy legs, grinning at me.

I knew where I was. I was in Slappy's dream. My plan had worked.

"The nightmare is over, Slappy," I said. "I won't be seeing you in my sleep anymore. No one will."

He tossed back his head and cackled. "How are you going to stop me, Richard?" he rasped.

"Like this," I said. I grabbed his jacket, slid my fingers into the pocket—and pulled out the folded-up sheet of paper.

"Hey—" he protested. He swiped at the page with one hand. Missed.

And I read the strange words out loud: "*Karru Marri Odonna Loma Molonu Karrano.*"

Slappy's mouth opened in a long, shrill scream.

And then the light began to dim. The dream faded. Slappy faded from sight. The blackness returned.

Did it work? Did I end Slappy's powers to invade dreams?

I tried to force myself awake. But I was in a deep sleep . . . a long, deep sleep.

When I finally blinked myself awake, I felt confused. *Where am I? Not in the lab? Am I back home?*

Yes. I gazed around the room. My bedroom. I was home. Sitting up on my bed.

I must have stayed asleep while Mom drove me home, I told myself.

I bumped my hands together. To my surprise, they made a *clonk* sound.

I gazed at my hands. I clapped them together.
Wood!

My hands were made of wood.

"Huh?" I gasped and slapped my forehead. My forehead was hard.

Wood!

"What is up with this?" I cried. My voice. I shouted in my voice as my wooden lips clicked up and down.

And then I saw myself in the dresser mirror against the wall.

"No. Oh noooo." I was Slappy. I was me, only I was inside the dummy.

And then Richard strolled to the bed and gazed down at me. "Hey, Dummy," he said—in Slappy's voice.

Slappy inside my body!

He tossed back his head and laughed his cold laugh to the ceiling.

"No!" I cried. "No!"

I banged my wooden hands on the bed.

Richard grinned at me. "Seems to have been a mix-up at the sleep lab," he rasped.

"No! Please—no!" I screamed.

Richard turned and started to leave the room. At the door, he turned back and called, in Slappy's voice, "Pleasant dreams, Dummy!"

EPILOGUE FROM SLAPPY

Hahahaha! I *love* a story with a happy ending—don't you?

Do you know what that dummy needs? A good night's sleep! Hahaha!

Maybe I'll call my next book *GUESS WHAT? I'M ALIVE!*

It's a dream come true for me.

And now I'm going to dream up another nightmare story for you.

Yes, I'll be back soon with another *Goosebumps* story.

Remember: This is *SlappyWorld.*

You only *scream* in it!

TWO HEADS ARE SCARIER THAN ONE!

SLAPPYWORLD #17:
HAUNTING WITH THE STARS

Turn the page for a sneak peek!

MARS, HERE I COME

By Murphy Shannon

My parents know that I think and dream about the planets and stars and outer space all the time. That's why they took me to the headquarters of the US Spaceship Academy for my birthday.

I was so excited, I couldn't sit still in the backseat of our car. I kept bumping up and down. I could barely breathe. This was the best birthday present ever!

But I didn't know how outstanding it would be.

I would love to work for the Spaceship Academy when I grow up. I know it's a wild dream. But maybe I could even be an astronaut and travel to another planet or circle the stars.

My friends Orly and Cleo think I'm weird. And maybe I am. But can you think of anything more exciting than being a space pioneer?

When we arrived at Spaceship Academy head-quarters, I leaped out of the car before Dad even finished parking. I stared up at the huge shiny building and cried out, "Wow!" The building reached up to the sky. It was all glass and shaped like a giant rocket ship.

Of course I'd seen videos about this place. But it didn't look this awesome on a screen. The building looked like it could blast off to space by itself!

Dad showed his special pass, and a guard in a uniform covered in shiny medals pressed some numbers on a keypad. The doors slid open for us. We stepped into an entry hall that had to be a mile long!

I felt dizzy staring at the models of spaceships that lined the center of the hall. Big posters of astronauts and photos from the moon and Mars covered the walls.

I wanted to stop and study each model spacecraft. But Mom said we had an appointment with an Academy captain, and we couldn't be late.

A Spaceship Academy captain! Whoa. Could this birthday get any more awesome?

We stopped in front of a glass office door. The name CAPTAIN FARRELL DODGE was stenciled in black letters on the door.

"Go in, Murphy," Dad said. "The appointment is only for you."

My hand was shaking as I pushed open the door and stepped inside. The office walls were covered with charts and maps of the galaxy.

Captain Dodge sat behind a big metal desk. He also had medals up and down his uniform jacket. A model of a spaceship stood on one corner of his desk.

He stood up and smiled as I entered. He was pretty young. Much younger than my parents, I think. "Hello, Murphy," he said. "I've been waiting to meet you." He stepped around the desk and shook my hand.

"Th-thank you," I stammered. I was too excited to say anything else.

I sat down in the chair across from his desk. He took his seat and leaned forward to talk to me. "Your parents wanted you to have a birthday surprise," he said, speaking in a low voice. "But they don't know the real reason I agreed to your visit."

I blinked. "Excuse me? The real reason?"

He nodded. "This is top secret, Murphy. The Spaceship Academy doesn't want to start a panic." His voice was just above a whisper.

"I—I don't understand," I replied.

"It's the Martians," he said. "We've heard rumors. Rumors they plan to attack."

"Huh? Martians?" I said.

He nodded again. "That's why we need you. We need you to go on a secret mission to Mars. We need you to find out if the rumors are true."

"But—but—I'm just a kid!" I cried. "I'm only twelve."

"Yes. That's why we need you," he said. "The Martians will expect someone from the military. But they'll never expect a kid."

I stared at him. My brain was spinning. "Are you serious?" I asked in a tiny voice.

He leaned closer over the desk and whispered, "Murphy, we need you to leave immediately. Will you do it?"

I finished reading my story and turned to Mom. "What do you think? Do you like it?"

Mom smiled. "I like it a lot, Murphy," she said.

"It's a very good start to a story. You are such a good writer. You take after me. I took creative writing in college."

"I think it's the best thing I've ever written," I said. "I can't wait to show it to Mr. Hawkins." I waved the story pages in my hand. "But I have one problem with it . . ."

"What's that?" Mom asked.

"There's no ending," I said. "It just stops."

"Yes. I was wondering about that," Mom said. "What happens next? Does Murphy go to Mars?"

I shrugged. "I don't know," I said. "I can't decide what happens next. I'm totally stumped."

Mom thought about it for a moment. "Well, tomorrow is your school trip to the Rayburne Observatory," she said. "You'll be looking at Mars and all the planets and stars in the big telescope. I'll bet that will give you some ideas for your story."

Mom wasn't always right. But she was right about that. My trip to the observatory gave me *lots* of ideas. *Terrifying* ideas.

Orly Roberts laughed and punched me in the leg. "Murphy, you're so excited, you can't breathe!" she said.

I shoved her fist away. "Hey, you know I have asthma. I always have to take this inhaler with me."

"You're totally pumped because you're going to see stars close-up," Cleo Lambeau said. "Look at you. You can't even sit still."

"I *am* sitting still," I said. "It's a bumpy road. The bus keeps bouncing me up and down."

The girls laughed. I sat between them as the school bus rumbled up the narrow mountain road. The three of us had been friends for a long time. You'd think they'd get tired of teasing me. But they don't.

The bus bounced hard. The inhaler flew out of my hand and dropped to the floor. Orly leaned over and picked it up for me.

I pointed out the window. "What's that animal? Did you see it? Was it a mountain lion?"

Cleo sat next to the window. "I think it was a

dog," she said. "Murphy, you're so psyched, you're seeing things!"

"You don't get it," I said. "This isn't a typical school trip. The Rayburne Observatory has one of the most powerful telescopes in the world."

"And you really think you're going to see close-ups of tiny Martians?" Orly said.

"And maybe they'll wave back at you," Cleo added. They both laughed.

"Do you know how funny you're *not*? You've seen too many cartoons," I said. "This is serious."

Serious to *me*, anyway. They could joke all they liked. But my parents took me to see a rocket blast off at NASA in Florida when I was nine, and I've been obsessed with stars and space travel and the universe ever since.

I dream about space travel. And I love writing stories about it.

Here's something I would never tell Orly or Cleo: My big dream is to be an astronaut.

I know. That's kind of sad. I don't think I'd ever be accepted. Mainly because I have asthma and bad allergies, and I have to carry the inhaler at all times.

But I can dream about it, right?

"Listen up, people." Mr. Hawkins, our sixth-grade teacher, stood up and faced us from the front of the bus. He's very tall, so he had to duck his head so he didn't hit the roof.

"We are approaching the observatory." He motioned out the window. "I just want to remind everyone that this is a place of serious science. You've had a long bus ride, and you're probably feeling restless. Like you want to run around and blow off steam."

He shook his head. "But you have to remember that many scientists are doing important work here. So, you need to be serious—and respectful, too—as we enter the observatory."

"Are we getting lunch?" Jesse Halstrom asked. Jesse always likes to know where his next meal is coming from.

"We will have lunch in the observatory cafeteria," Mr. Hawkins said.

"Will it be that freeze-dried astronaut stuff?" Jesse asked.

A lot of kids laughed.

"I think they serve real food," the teacher answered. "As you remember from the videos we watched, the observatory is enormous. Please stick together. Do not wander off on your own. I can't keep track of all of you. And when we return to school, I'd like to bring most of you back with me."

That was a joke. And we all laughed really hard because Mr. Hawkins doesn't make that many jokes.

The bus climbed higher and squealed around a curve. And I could see the huge stone building poking up from the trees above us. My heart started to pound as I gazed at the enormous dome, gleaming under the sunlight.

Orly grabbed my arm. "Your breathing is like an accordion going in and out!" she said. "Calm down."

"We're only going to *see* stars and planets," Cleo said. "We're not going to *visit* them."

She was wrong.

2

We piled off the bus and followed a gray-uniformed guard through the wide glass front doors and into a huge round entryway. Our footsteps echoed off the high stone ceilings.

"This is awesome!" I whispered to Orly and Cleo.

Cleo rolled her eyes. "I thought you might say that."

We heard rapid footsteps ringing out on the marble floor. A man in a long white lab coat came walking out. And I gasped. "It's *him*! It's Sidney Rayburne! I don't believe it. He actually came to greet us himself!"

Cleo raised a finger to her lips. "Murphy, please. You're going to explode if you don't calm down!"

Dr. Rayburne was tall and thin with straight white hair pulled back in a ponytail. He had pale blue eyes behind black square-framed eyeglasses and a white mustache that stuck straight out at the sides. He carried a clipboard in one hand, which he swung as he stepped in front of the class.

I'd read a lot about Sidney Rayburne, but I never expected to be in the same room with him.

He designed the amazing telescope that made him famous around the world. And he was in charge of the observatory and all the scientists who worked here.

Some videos I saw said that he was a bit strange and didn't always get along with other astronomers. A lot of people said he was difficult to work with.

He shook hands with Mr. Hawkins, and they said a few words to each other. I was desperate to shake hands with him, too. I knew I would never wash that hand!

He turned to us, and a smile formed beneath the straight mustache. "I am always happy to greet school classes here in my observatory," he said. He had a deep, booming voice that rang off the stone walls. "And I promise you that you will see parts of the universe you have never seen."

"How far can the telescope see in the daytime?" I asked. I couldn't help it. I couldn't hold back my question. My voice came out high and shrill because of my excitement.

"It's the same day or night. My assistants will be explaining everything you want to know," Rayburne replied. "I'm sure that you—"

"How many other galaxies have you seen?" I blurted out.

Rayburne chuckled. "I hope we can answer all your questions later, young man."

"I read that the Salzburg telescope was designed to be more powerful than yours," I said. "Is it true?"

Mr. Hawkins took a few steps toward me. "Murphy, if you could hold your questions till later . . ."

Cleo squeezed my arm hard. "Shhh. What's your problem?"

"Murphy Shannon is a bit of a fanatic," I heard Hawkins tell Dr. Rayburne. "This is the biggest day of his life."

Rayburne's smile grew wide. "I know we won't disappoint you, Murphy."

He gave us a quick wave. "Enjoy your trip to the stars, everyone." Then he turned and walked out of the room.

Two women in white lab coats appeared and led the class into a large, round auditorium. Tiny lights twinkled like stars, high overhead in the domed ceiling. Comfortable movie-theater seats wrapped around the wide circle.

"I am Dr. Gonzalez, and this is Dr. Jackson," one of the women announced. "Sit anywhere you like." She motioned around the circle with one hand. "Our chief astronomer, Dr. Freed, will be here to give you an introduction to the observatory."

I led Cleo and Orly to the back row because it had the best view of the entire ceiling. "This is awesome!" I said. "I'll bet they have amazing light shows up there on the dome."

"Murphy, take a deep breath," Cleo said. "You've really got to chill."

"I hope this astronomer will let us ask questions," I said. "I have a million things I want to know about this place."

"If you have any problem," Dr. Gonzalez said, "or if you need to leave the auditorium for any reason, please see Dr. Jackson or me. Because of security, you will need a guide wherever you go."

Around the room, everyone began talking at once. I wasn't the only kid who was excited. But, of course, I was the *most* excited.

The room grew quiet as Dr. Freed, a tall young man in a dark suit, came stepping into the middle of the circle. He had wavy black hair down to his shoulders, and a short black beard covered most of his face. He wore a red bandanna around his neck in place of a tie, and I saw a silver ring gleam in one ear.

Freed had a tiny microphone clipped to the lapel of his suit jacket, which he tested by poking a finger against it. "Testing . . . testing . . . one . . . two . . . three . . ."

Dr. Gonzalez carried a tall wooden stool to the center of the circle. Dr. Freed lowered himself to the edge of the seat and cleared his throat. "Welcome, everyone," he said. "I am Samuel Freed, and I'm the head astronomer here at the Rayburne Observatory."

He fiddled with the microphone for a few seconds. "We have clear weather on the mountaintop today," he continued. "So I know you kids are going to have some amazing views later."

"Oh, wow," I murmured. I was forcing myself to stay calm. But that was definitely good news.

"I'd like to start out by giving you all a brief history of the telescope," Freed said. As he said that, the twinkling stars disappeared from the domed ceiling. A photo of an old-fashioned telescope took their place. All the other lights in the auditorium went dark.

"In 1609," Dr. Freed continued, "an Italian astronomer named Galileo became the first person to use a telescope aimed at the stars. Even though his telescope was small and primitive, Galileo was able to make out mountains and craters on the moon. In later years . . ."

Freed rattled on about Galileo and Sir Isaac Newton and how telescopes became bigger and sharper. He had a droning voice, and he was reciting everything as if he had said it all a hundred times before.

I poked Cleo in the side. "Come on," I whispered. "I already know all this stuff. Let's get out of here."

Her mouth dropped open. "Sneak out? No way. You heard what they said—"

I motioned to the door right behind us. "Let's just take a short walk. You know. Explore. While he's doing ancient history."

"I'm with you," Orly said. "This is boring."

Cleo crossed her arms in front of her. "I'm not going. They said not to leave."

I grabbed both of them by the arm and tugged them to their feet. I was too excited to sit still. I pulled them to the door, and we slipped out.

"A short walk," I whispered. "Very short. No one will notice we're gone."

Was I making a mistake?

3

"Let go of my arm. I don't want to do this," Cleo said.

Orly was always ready to have fun. But Cleo was the wimp in the group. She was a genius at finding things to be afraid of, like always finding bugs in her food that turned out to be raisins or chocolate chips.

She never went bike riding with Orly and me because "what if I got a flat tire?" When she was home by herself, she turned on every light in the house. I'm not sure why.

Last summer when my parents took the three of us to the beach, Orly and I went racing into the waves. It was so cold, we started to scream.

Cleo stood on the edge of the water, pointing: "Look out! I think I see jellyfish!"

The three of us have been friends for so long, Orly and I don't give Cleo a hard time about being afraid and timid. And I don't know. Maybe it's good to have one friend who is sometimes the sensible one.

I let go of Cleo's arm. "We'll just take a short

walk outside the auditorium," I said. "A minute or two. That's all. Just to stretch our legs."

"You need to stretch your brain," Cleo said. "We don't belong out here."

I pointed up and down the hall. "There's no one here. They must all be in the different labs doing their jobs."

The endless hallway had a dark marble floor and solid stone walls. Wide wooden doors lined the outer wall. They were all closed. The air was cold and smelled sharply of detergent.

I could hear Dr. Freed's droning voice from the loudspeakers in the auditorium. I led the way to the left. "Come on. This is an adventure."

"I don't like adventure," Cleo grumbled. "You know what adventure means? It means trouble."

"It's so quiet out in this hall, you can hear the air," Orly said. She stared up ahead. "There's an open door. Let's see what's there."

Cleo held back, but Orly and I trotted to the open doorway. It opened into a brightly lit room with several glass display cases.

I gazed from wall to wall. They were covered with huge maps. "They're all maps of the universe, I think."

I made my way to the nearest display case. Spread out under the glass was an ancient yellowed scroll. It had the faded outline of an island or maybe a continent on it.

"It must be really old," Orly said, gazing down at it. "Like maybe one of the first-ever maps."

"They should put labels on these maps to identify them," I said.

"They're not really on display, Murphy," Cleo said. "This is a private room, remember? We're not supposed to be in here."

I ignored her and moved to the next case. "This looks like a map of North America," I said. "But the writing all over it is in a foreign language."

"Awesome," Orly murmured.

"Can we go back?" Cleo asked, tugging my arm.

"One more room," I said. "I promise. Just one more room."

We went back into the hall and followed it, passing several more closed doors. I could hear voices behind some of the doors and the hum of large machines.

Another open door revealed a tall glass case in the middle of a brightly lit room. I blinked and gazed at the planets that appeared to be floating inside the case.

"Wow," I muttered. "Check it out. Do you recognize it? It's our galaxy."

Orly stepped up to the glass. "It's in 3-D," she said.

"It's a hologram of the galaxy," I said. "Amazing."

Cleo gasped. "Oh no!"

And then I heard it, too. Footsteps. The click of footsteps approaching the room.

No time to duck or hide. All three of us spun to the door as a woman hurried in. I recognized her from the auditorium. Dr. Jackson.

Her expression grew grim as she eyed us in front of the glass case.

"I—I—I—" I stammered. I couldn't think of an excuse for why we were there.

She raised a finger to her lips. "Listen to me," she said in a choked whisper. She glanced behind her, as if she expected someone to be there.

Suddenly, I realized she looked frightened.

"I'm sorry," I said. "I know we shouldn't—"

"Listen to me," she repeated. "I can only say it once." She glanced behind her again. "Get out of here."

"Okay," I said. "We'll go back. We'll—"

"No!" she cried. "Get out of here. Go home. Get the others and go home . . . while you still have the chance."

My mouth dropped open. Cleo uttered a low cry.

I heard voices out in the hall.

"Dr. Jackson—" I started. But she spun around, her eyes wide with fear, and ran from the room.

The three of us stood frozen in front of the tall glass case. "W-why did she say that?" I stammered.

"She was just trying to scare us," Orly replied.

Cleo raised her hands to her cheeks. "But why? Why did she want to scare us? And why did she say that and then just run away?"

"She knew we didn't belong in here," I said. "And so—"

"So she decided to frighten us to death?" Cleo demanded.

I could see that Orly was thinking hard. "Cleo is right. It's totally strange. Why didn't she take us back to the auditorium?"

I shrugged. "Who knows?" I started to the door. "We'd better get back. Maybe she won't squeal on us."

We stepped into the hallway. In the distance, I saw two women in white lab coats disappear around the curve. I froze and waited to make sure they weren't returning.

"Which way do we go?" Cleo asked. "I got turned around." She shook her head. "I *knew* we'd get lost."

"We're not lost," Orly told her. "We just don't know where we are."

That didn't cheer Cleo up.

Orly motioned to the right. "Isn't that the way we came?"

I gazed in both directions. "No," I said. "I think we came from the other direction."

I led the way. The girls kept shaking their heads. "This doesn't feel right," Cleo whispered.

We passed a few closed doors. A stenciled sign next to a wide glass door read LIBRARY.

"We definitely didn't pass a library," Cleo said. Her voice trembled.

Orly squeezed her hand. "You're shaking. We'll be okay, Cleo. Even if we're lost, we can still—"

"We're not lost," I snapped. "Follow me." We started back toward the galaxy hologram room. "The auditorium should be on our left," I whispered. "We just have to find an entrance."

Cleo shook her head. "I can't believe we did this." Her voice sounded hollow in the long hallway. "All because Murphy wanted an adventure."

"Go ahead. Blame me," I said. "It's not like I forced you two to come."

"Yes, you did," Cleo said.

"Please, don't argue," Orly said. "Let's get back and pretend this didn't happen. We—"

She stopped. We all heard the thud of footsteps. Nearby.

"Over here," I whispered. We burst through an open doorway. The room had bright overhead lights. I saw a tower of computer monitors against the far wall. Laptops, scanners, all kinds of computer equipment.

We darted farther into the room and pressed ourselves against the near wall. My heart was pounding so hard, my breath came out in quick wheezes. I kept my back tight against the wall, the two girls beside me.

We listened as the footsteps passed. "We settled on Florida because it's nearby," a man said.

"And the weather is so nice there," said a woman walking with him.

When their voices faded, I let out a long sigh of relief. "That was close," I said.

"Very close!" a deep voice said from across the room.

I gasped and raised my eyes. We weren't alone.

A gray-haired man in a tan suit stepped out from behind a tall file cabinet.

"Ohhh." Orly let out a startled groan. Cleo stayed pressed against the wall, her eyes wide with fright.

"What are you kids doing in here?" the man demanded. "This room is forbidden to all visitors."

"We—uh—we—" I struggled to speak.

He picked up some kind of radio transmitter and raised it to his face. "Security! Security!" he shouted into it. "Intruders in 1214. Security!"

About the Author

R.L. Stine says he gets to scare people all over the world. So far, his books have sold more than 400 million copies, making him one of the most popular children's authors in history. The Goosebumps series has more than 150 titles and has inspired a TV series and two motion pictures. R.L. himself is a character in the movies! He has also written the teen series Fear Street, and the Mostly Ghostly and Nightmare Room series. He is currently writing a series of graphic novels entitled Just Beyond. R.L. Stine lives in New York City with his wife, Jane, an editor and publisher. You can learn more about him at rlstine.com.

Catch the MOST WANTED Goosebumps® villains UNDEAD OR ALIVE!

SPECIAL EDITIONS

SCHOLASTIC

scholastic.com/goosebumps

GBMW42

REVENGE OF THE LIVING DUMMY
R.L. STINE
SCHOLASTIC

CREEP FROM THE DEEP
R.L. STINE
SCHOLASTIC

MONSTER BLOOD FOR BREAKFAST!
R.L. STINE
SCHOLASTIC

THE SCREAM OF THE HAUNTED MASK
R.L. STINE
SCHOLASTIC

DR. MANIAC VS. ROBBY SCHWARTZ
R.L. STINE
SCHOLASTIC

WHO'S YOUR MUMMY?
R.L. STINE
SCHOLASTIC

MY FRIENDS CALL ME MONSTER
R.L. STINE
SCHOLASTIC

SAY CHEESE - AND DIE SCREAMING!
R.L. STINE
SCHOLASTIC

WELCOME TO CAMP SLITHER
R.L. STINE
SCHOLASTIC

SCHOLASTIC

www.scholastic.com/goosebumps

GBHL19H2

R. L. Stine's Fright Fest!
Now with Splat Stats and More!

THE ORIGINAL Goosebumps BOOKS
WITH AN ALL-NEW LOOK!

R.L. Stine's
Biography

GET YOUR HANDS ON THEM BEFORE THEY GET THEIR HANDS ON YOU!

CONTINUE THE FRIGHT
AT THE GOOSEBUMPS SITE
scholastic.com/goosebumps

FANS OF GOOSEBUMPS CAN:

- PLAY THE GHOULISH GAME:
  GOOSEBUMPS: SLAPPY'S DROP DEAD HOUSE

- LEARN ABOUT NEW BOOKS AND TERRIFYING CLASSICS

- TAKE A QUIZ AND LEARN WHICH TYPE OF MONSTER YOU ARE!

- LEARN ABOUT THE AUTHOR WHO STARTED IT ALL: R.L. STINE

SCHOLASTIC

GBWEB2019

THE *Goosebumps* SERIES COMES TO LIFE IN A BRAND-NEW DIGITAL WORLD

MEET Slappy—and explore the *Goosebumps* Zone.
PLAY games, create an avatar, and chat with other fans.

Start your adventure today! Download the **HOME BASE** app and scan this image to unlock exclusive rewards!

SCHOLASTIC.COM/HOMEBASE

Goosebumps SLAPPYWORLD

THIS IS SLAPPY'S WORLD—
YOU ONLY SCREAM IN IT!

SLAPPY BIRTHDAY TO YOU
R.L. STINE

ATTACK OF THE JACK!
R.L. STINE

I AM SLAPPY'S EVIL TWIN
R.L. STINE

PLEASE DO NOT FEED THE WEIRDO
R.L. STINE

ESCAPE FROM SHUDDER MANSION
R.L. STINE

THE GHOST OF SLAPPY
R.L. STINE

IT'S ALIVE! IT'S ALIVE!
R.L. STINE

THE DUMMY MEETS THE MUMMY!
R.L. STINE

REVENGE OF THE INVISIBLE BOY!
R.L. STINE

DIARY OF A DUMMY
R.L. STINE

THEY CALL ME THE NIGHT HOWLER!
R.L. STINE

MY FRIEND SLAPPY
R.L. STINE

MONSTER BLOOD IS BACK
R.L. STINE

THE HAUNTED ZOMBIE
R.L. STINE

JUDY AND THE BEAST
R.L. STINE

SLAPPY IN DREAMLAND
R.L. STINE

SCHOLASTIC

GBSLAPPYWORLD16